I0822513

Annabel

Or the [*sexual*] *Adventures of a Good Girl*

Brigitte Roick

Order this book online at www.trafford.com
or email orders@trafford.com

Most Trafford titles are also available at major online book retailers.

Cover by Mary Peppard
Peppardigital@shaw.ca

Printed in Victoria, BC, Canada.

ISBN: 978-1-4269-0084-6 (soft)
ISBN: 978-1-4269-0085-3 (hard)
ISBN: 978-1-4269-0086-0 (ebook)

Trafford rev. 4/21/2010

www.trafford.com

North America & international
toll-free: 1 888 232 4444 (USA & Canada)
phone: 250 383 6864 • fax: 812 355 4082

*T*his book is dedicated to all the handsome, charming, and oh so irresistible men who never knew I existed – but who made love to me at night, in my dreams.

Prologue

When I was a little girl I knew, once I was grown up, I would marry my father. My mother had died when I was two, and my Papa, who raised me and my older brother, had become my adored hero. I simply couldn't imagine a life without being close to him. Little did I know that another force, called sex drive, would shatter my dreams. My father remarried. I was fourteen, and my idyllic world collapsed. From being daddy's darling my position altered to being in constant fights with my stepmother for his attention. Naturally I lost. It was my imagination that saved me.

My father, an engineer and director of the gas works, hadn't been drafted into Hitler's army; our little town in Westfalia hadn't been important enough to be bombed, and apart from food shortages, my daily life had continued in routine fashion. Until that wicked stepmother, straight out of *Hänsel und Gretel*, turned my world upside down.

During the Nazi reign there were no foreign movies, no foreign books that might open your mind, and there was no foreign music. The only accepted entertainment for children were the fairy tales by the Brothers Grimm and Hans Christian Andersen. I read them, watched actors perform them on stage, and sat spellbound in our community hall when once a month a film was shown and the impossible fairy tale tasks became celluloid reality. My imagination started to soar like the eleven brothers when their wicked stepmother turns them into swans, and I was driven into the profession where make-believe was born.

Chapter 1

1952 - 53

My carnal knowledge was sketchy – like that of most young girls in those days. To tell the truth, I didn't know what carnal meant – at seventeen years of age! My sex education had consisted of my stepmother, who turned out to be less wicked than simple, telling me that babies grew under a woman's heart. I had been curious about the big round tummy a woman in our neighbourhood was trying to conceal under a tent-like dress. At fifteen I had asked my brother, who was five years older than I, why sex was such a hush hush affair? His answer had been brief. 'You'll find out when you are old enough. Just make sure you don't get pregnant.'

Sex was a puzzle, but I knew about love. I had seen people steal for it, become ill over it, and die for it in films and novels. When the screen couple, after a passionate kiss, was slowly sliding into a horizontal position, and the camera focussed on a willow tree whose branches were swaying and sighing in the wind, I sensed that something exciting must be happening – but what? I had noticed crude, vulgar drawings in public washrooms and tried not to look at them. They disgusted me! Surely they had nothing to do with love and its fulfillment!

In my last year in high school I experienced love for the first time with a real flesh-and-blood young man who was about to graduate. His name was Roman and he was more handsome than any movie star I had previously worshipped. He was tall and had a mane of dark, gently curled hair. His name suited him. He could have been a general in Caesar's army crossing the Alps in stormy weather – his dark curls powdered with snow. He, and the entire student body, had watched me in a play our ambitious French teacher had produced. The teacher had cast me as a high-spirited young boy who got into all sorts of trouble. My performance rewarded me with a passing mark in French and encouraging praise from all the teachers and students. I was bathing in self-confidence and self-importance. My destiny had been decided for me! I would be an actress – a glorious career on stage and in films was awaiting me.

The day after the performance, Roman stopped me while I was running back to my class after recess.

'You've got talent girl', he said. 'I wonder if you can do me a favour. My class is planning to put on a show to celebrate the end of our school days. There is a part for a girl in one of the sketches. Would you like to do it?'

'Sure, I would love to!' Instantly I saw myself in Roman's arms in a passionate love scene. 'If you think I'm right for the part,' I added in a subdued voice.

A week after our conversation I had my first rehearsal.

'Do you have a script for me,' I asked Roman.

'I don't think you need one – I'll tell you what to do when we get to it.'

I waited – my heart pounding in my chest. I slipped a peppermint into my mouth and wiped my sweaty palms on my handkerchief. I watched two of his classmates rehearsing a dialogue on stage. Roman was sitting in the front row, directing. I hadn't dared to sit down beside him, but had chosen the seat directly behind. Suddenly he turned around.

'This is your cue, Anna. When Harold turns his back to the audience, you walk slowly, but not too slowly, across the stage.'

That's all he wanted me for? Any girl could have filled that part! My romantic dream evaporated like a puddle in the sunshine. Roman must have read my mind.

'Sorry Anna, but this girl has to be quite pretty, that's why I chose you.' I felt consoled. Now I was sure he was attracted to me.

I had one more rehearsal, and then the night of the performance. There was going to be a dance afterwards. I dreamed of Roman's arms holding me tight, and dancing, dancing the night away in his embrace.

'One of you young men will have to take Anna home,' our school principal, who was in charge of the event, announced after the performance. 'We can't let her walk in the dark without an escort.'

Roman, please, Roman . . . oh my good fairy, please make it Roman!

'I'll take her,' Harold rushed to put on his coat. 'Will I do?'

No, no, you stupid bastard – not you! You are spoiling everything!

I felt like kicking him in the shins! Instead I weakly nodded approval.

Outside on the dark road, he took my arm and pulled it through his. He talked about his plans for the future . . . yak . . . yak . . . yak . . . on and on. I didn't say a single word. I was so mad.

'You are a pretty girl, Anna,' he said when we reached my house. 'I want to give you a kiss.' Before I could answer he pulled me into his arms and kissed me on the mouth.

'Good night, fair lady,' he called as he walked away. 'Sweet dreams.'

I had a nightmare! Roman and I were dancing in some kind of hall when suddenly a whole gang of students, all girls, came tearing in, jerked Roman out of my arms and pulled him away with them. I tried to follow the crowd but my feet wouldn't move. I screamed, 'Roman, Roman help' – and woke myself up.

It was easy to forget Roman. He had been an out-of-town student and I never saw him again. I was free to focus all my energies on my dream. After a couple of restless nights I had it all figured out. First item on my agenda was my father. I had to convince him that an acting career was the only path I could pursue. He would have to agree that a talent like mine was God given, and not to be wasted.

I caught him in one of his joyful moods after Sunday dinner. My stepmother had produced a juicy pork roast, dumplings that had maintained their lightness, and Sauerkraut cooked to perfection – soft, and flavoured with apples and onions. She was a good cook I had to admit. But weren't witches famous for their enticing brews?

'May I join you on your walk, Papa,' I asked him after I had done my job of clearing the table. My stepmother had told me in the morning that she would be visiting her friend next door in the afternoon. A new family had moved in across the road, and there was a lot of gossip about the couple. There were two names on their nameplate below the bell. Maybe they weren't married? I knew my stepmama and her friend would have a field day gossiping about the newcomers. I would have my father to myself for at least a couple of hours.

'Papa, I have decided what I want to be.' I had taken his arm and we were strolling along the narrow path that led into the nearby forest – our favourite Sunday afternoon route.

'About time, Anna,' my father stopped and looked at me. 'I hope it's something sensible.'

'Oh, it is!' I shouted. 'And it is exciting and creative, and I can make a lot of money, and you'll be ever so proud of me when you see me on stage or in a movie . . .'

'You want to be an actress?' My father's voice took on a new sound. For a second my courage left me – his eyes were pinned on me with such severity.

'I . . . have the talent . . . everybody in school said so, even all the teachers . . . and Pastor Seibert said if you have a God given talent you are obligated to develop it and . . .' I searched frantically for another angle that would appeal to him. 'Imagine yourself as the father of a famous actress, sought after by all major theatres and film studios . . . imagine sitting in a movie theatre and your own daughter appears on the screen, in a close-up . . . imagine how your friends and all the men in the gas works would envy you . . .' The last argument was a good one. It aimed at my father's vanity, at his own desire to stand out, to be special. He hadn't been able to achieve preferred status in our community as an engineer at the gas works. I knew how undervalued he felt.

'But so many young girls have that dream, Anna. The competition is enormous.' His voice sounded much softer now. I had hit a tender chord. 'And wouldn't you want to marry one day? Actresses have a certain reputation – I don't think a solid businessman, or a professional man would want to marry an actress . . .'

'That's where you are wrong, Papa,' I cut him off. 'What about Rita Hayworth and Aga Khan? She is a princess now –

and rich – and anyway, I don't want to marry . . . I mean not yet.' I added the last part to reassure him. I had no intention of telling him my secret plans.

Marriage didn't appeal to me – no, not at all. I had observed so many bad ones. My parents were a good example. My father was interested in soccer and all outdoor activities – my stepmother was a homebody. She got a kick out of the purchase of a new tablecloth because, imagine, it matched the curtains in the dining room! The two of them were about as different as a mouse and a lion. I often felt sorry for both of them. And there were our neighbours, the Meyers. Some time ago Herr Meyer had been involved, the rumour went, with another woman. His wife punished him by talking to him in a condescending tone, like she talked to her children, right in front of everybody. How pitiful! And my brother Hans, married for one year only, was complaining about his wife every time he visited with us. She was burning his dinners, she couldn't iron his shirts, she hovered over him when he came home from work, tired, wanting nothing but peace.

Poor Hans, marriage had changed him so much. He no longer got a kick out of teasing me, telling me silly jokes, or spending a night at the pub with his old friends from school. He talked about money and bills, and that he wasn't ready for a child. Christa, his wife, was expecting. Gone were the days when, at village dances, pretty girls were practically lining up at his table, eager to snatch a dance with him – gone the times when he spent his holidays climbing the highest mountains in the Bavarian Alps, or diving in the North Sea for sunken submarines. My father, I noticed, was pleased with the change in him. He proudly remarked how marriage had finally matured his son. I believe he secretly thought: Why should you escape the trap I'm caught in, my boy.

My father's daughter, I was going to make sure, would not be trapped. Soon as I had decided to become an actress, I had put in a special order at our bookshop for a biography of Sarah Bernhardt, who was regarded as the greatest actress ever. What a life she had lived! How many important men had knelt at her feet! Just to be invited into her dressing room had been a triumph for them. I imagined myself in a lacy negligee, my hair falling wild and untamed across my face, my dresser hovering over me, ready to help me into an expensive gown, and handsome, distinguished men knocking at my door, eager to hand me bouquets of flowers. I would love them all, and marry none.

Chapter 2

1954 –1956

I had conquered my father. He had succumbed to my wishes though he insisted I study at the Max Reinhardt Drama School in Berlin, and board with my grandmother. 'The idea of you living in a rented room in the divided city is out of the question. Your grandmother will look after you – you won't be alone,' he reasoned. I didn't mind my grandmother - my step grandmother to be correct. She was the only grandparent I had and I thought she was alright, for an old lady. She had visited us on several occasions, and I had taken to calling her Oma. The thing that bothered me was being looked after. I wanted to get away from any supervision! I wanted to be free, do what I pleased, conquer the world!

At the train station I kissed my Papa good-bye and promised him to be a good girl. 'Remember who you are and where you come from,' he said. 'Listen to Oma. She's been through a lot in her life. Trust her judgment.' I said I would.

As I was about to board the train, my stepmama pulled me back by my coat. 'Don't trust men, Anna, young or old,' she whispered in my ear. 'They have only one thing in mind – and you are too young for that. Make sure you are never alone with a man.' I assured her I would.

I found a seat beside a middle-aged woman in a fur coat. The coat had bare patches and reminded me of our cat Rumpel, short for Rumpelstiltskin. When he got into a fight, fur went flying. He had ended up with bare patches more than once, and my stepmama had threatened him with house arrest. My timid Mama . . . her remark at the station made me smile . . . she was so right! Older men weren't as harmless as they made you believe. I remembered an incident at my graduation ball. My stepmother's dressmaker had produced a soft lilac taffeta gown for the occasion, as the only clothing store in our town didn't carry party dresses. I felt quite elegant and grown up in my long, rustling gown. Our German teacher, who was at least forty, asked me for a dance. He appreciated my acting talent and had always asked me to read aloud the poems we were studying – long, classical poems by Goethe and Schiller. He held me close and tight on the dance floor, and when the music stopped, he walked me back to our table, very slowly, holding onto my hand. Before he let go, he squeezed my hand and looked into my eyes. I held his gaze and squeezed him right back. A strange current seemed to connect us – strange, but exciting.

I was pulled out of my reverie when the train stopped. The people in my compartment started to slide the books they had been reading into their coat pockets, and the fur-coated lady slid something into her coat's inner lining. The atmosphere felt tense. We had reached Helmstedt, the border town. From here the train crossed into Eastern Germany, the *Deutsche Demokratische Republik* or DDR for short. Everybody knew that it was neither a democracy nor a republic.

We heard heavy footsteps in the gangway and the forceful opening and closing of compartment doors. A young man in a mud-coloured uniform entered our space – a member of the *Volkspolizei*. Nobody said a word. He asked for our identity cards. He checked each one at length. He looked at our baggage on the rack, then pulled my suitcase down. He asked a man to get up so he could rest the suitcase on his seat. The man obliged instantly. He opened my case and rummaged through its contents. Finally he pulled out an item, shook it out, and held it up with two hands. I held my breath. It was a see-through negligée. I had sewn it myself, secretly in my room, from a pair of sheer curtains. It was a copy of the garment Rita Hayworth had worn in *The Seven Veils*. The young *Volkspolizist* looked at me and grinned. 'Capitalist decadence,' he muttered. He crushed it into a ball and slid it into his pocket. 'Confiscated!' He marched out of the compartment and closed the door with a bang.

The tense silence in our little space was broken by laughter. 'Not so loud,' the fur-coated lady warned. But she couldn't stop the outburst. One man tried so hard not to laugh out loud his head turned flame red. I thought it might explode. 'You made my day,' he blubbered between laughs. 'Young woman, are you in the fashion business?' I grabbed the lifeline he had thrown me. 'I'm . . . going to be . . . a fashion designer,' I said. 'I'll attend art school in Berlin.' Luckily I didn't have to look at him. I was busy closing up my suitcase and attempting to heave it back onto the rack. He got up and helped me. 'You have talent,' he whispered, 'maybe you can design one for my wife?' I giggled politely and thanked him for his help.

We arrived in Berlin without another stop. West German trains were not allowed to stop in the DDR. I don't think anybody would have wanted them to. Most of the buildings we passed had looked run-down, and others, in the towns, were still in ruins from the war.

A sigh of relief was heard when the train pulled into Bahnhof Zoo in West Berlin. I couldn't believe the hustle and bustle. People and luggage and trolleys crowded the platform. How was I going to find my grandmother? My eyes caught a bright blue hat adorned with a long white feather as it wobbled through the crowd. The fashions women wore in the big city! Outrageous! The crowd around the hat cleared as people descended down the stairs to the exit.

'Oma, it's you!' I shouted. 'Where did you get that hat . . .'

'I wouldn't want to be caught dead in it,' she smiled. 'But I knew it would catch your attention . . . you're not used to the traffic in a big city. I was afraid you might panic if you didn't find me.'

We walked out of the station carrying my heavy suitcase between us.

'We'll take the bus,' Oma announced. 'It'll give you a chance to see a bit of the city.' As the bus snaked its way from stop to stop my eyes picked out buildings still in ruins and others clad in scaffolding.

'You should have seen the place right after the war,' Oma commented. 'There wasn't a house standing for many blocks in some areas. Give it a couple more years and all ruins will be gone. The Americans are pumping in big dollars. They want to show the Communists how much better life is in the Western sector. You'll be surprised when you see the Kurfürstendamm . . . the stores . . . and the cafés, as good as before the war.'

After half an hour's drive we had to get off the bus and board a streetcar. Oma had been fortunate to live in a suburb. Few bombs had done damage there, no fighting had taken place, and best of all, it had become the American sector when the city was divided. I realized the advantages but I dreaded the long commute I would have to my school.

More dread seeped into my mind when we arrived at her home. Oma's flat was on the second floor of a long, narrow, three-storey apartment block which sat back from the road.

There was a grassy area in the front, bordered by a row of young trees. Farther up the street I spotted single houses with proper front gardens. It reminded me of home. I was glad I wouldn't be surrounded by bricks and concrete, busy roads and store fronts. My anxiety returned when we entered the building. There were dirty patches and scratches on the painted walls in the hall. I entered her flat not knowing what to expect. The walls were clean, the furniture acceptable, and my room contained a big, cozy looking bed and a heavy, old-fashioned armoire. A Persian kind of rug covered the floor. I walked to the window, pulled the curtains aside – and looked right into a graveyard. A crow was sitting on an elaborate gravestone croaking, screeching – making that unpleasant, unmelodious noise. Was that a bad omen? Suddenly a cool breeze blew through the window. Goose bumps formed on my bare arms. What was I doing here? What had I done? My dream seemed a pathetic fantasy – a whim, a figment of my imagination! I wrapped my arms around my chest and kept looking at the gravestones. The crow croaked again - loud and ugly. 'I'll show you!' I screamed at it. 'You are not going to scare me!' I rushed to the door.

'I'll be back in a minute,' I called out to my grandmother who was preparing supper in the kitchen. 'Just going to visit with my new neighbours in the back.'

The big, iron gate moaned when I opened it. The crow, my bad omen, took flight. I was enveloped in silence. Rows and rows of gravestones, some old and weathered, others clean and new. I stopped at a fresh grave. Bunches of wilting flowers littered the site. I read the inscription on the modest stone. Annabel Hamel, 1934 – 1954. She was born the same year as I – and dead. What dreams had she dreamed? What had she wanted to achieve in her life? Whatever it was, she hadn't been given a chance. But I had! I was alive and strong and able to make my dream come true. Annabel – that's what I would call myself. No more Anna banana - a tease my brother had invented - I would be Annabel Lambert. I couldn't change my family name – for my father's sake. But I could pronounce it the French way, Lam*bert* – Annabel Lam*bert*. It sounded as intriguing as Sarah Bernhardt, as musical as Madame Pompadour and as exciting as Brigitte Bardot, the new French siren's name. That night I fell asleep whispering my new name: Annabel Lam*bert* - Annabel Lam*bert* - Annabel the Divine . . .

Chapter 3

'Anna, I see your fee is paid – you can start classes tomorrow.' The secretary, a grey-haired woman with thick glasses looked up from her papers. Her big protruding eyes and her wrinkled skin reminded me of a toad. Was that another bad omen?

'Annabel,' I whispered, subdued by her intense glance. 'My name is Annabel.'

'It says Anna on your registration. Let's keep it that way. It's shorter.'

She handed me a timetable. 'We like punctuality at the drama school. This morning you are an hour late.'

She was right. I hadn't allowed enough time for the commute. Oma had told me which bus to use and where I had to transfer. It's a long way, she had said – not how long. I had no idea that Tegel was at the northernmost end of the Western sector and Grunewald at the most southern – a distance of some twenty, maybe thirty kilometres! To make things worse I had missed my connecting bus because I had been waiting on the wrong side of the road. The traffic on the streets made it hazardous to cross. I stood on the sidewalk hoping for a gap in the endless flow of cars. After a couple of minutes, a young woman stopped beside me. She looked to the left and to the right and plunged straight into the danger zone. I had enough presence of mind to follow right behind her. A couple of cars blew their horns at us. The woman slowed her steps and turned around. 'Don't worry,' she said, 'they always do that.' Two more angry blasts of a horn! The woman smiled at the closest driver. He raised his arms up to heaven and shouted something – no doubt something nasty. She rewarded him with a graceful wave of her arm, like she was the Queen of England acknowledging her subjects, and moved on. When my bus arrived, the queue of people started to push its way in. I waited till the rush was over – and was left standing on the sidewalk. The driver closed the door right in my face. When at last I found myself on the street I was looking for, I was sure I had the wrong address. The street was tree-lined on both sides – it allowed only a glimpse of big old houses squatting in vast, well-kept gardens. No sign of a school! I studied the house numbers, and there it was! A small brass sign by the door read *Max-Reinhardt-Schule des Landes Berlin.* I stood in front of a beautiful mansion with marble stairs leading to the double entrance doors. What an exciting surprise! Unfortunately, my travel venture made me an hour late – as the secretary had pointed out.

Scanning our classes for the week, I was impressed by the variety. I hadn't expected fencing and French to be part of our training. I was delighted. French, fencing - how romantic that sounded! The biggest chunk of time though was allotted to role study. There were four drama coaches – apparently well-known actors in Berlin, though I had never heard of them. I was eager to meet them, study with them, learn from them.

When I was about to leave for home, a short young man, who looked like one of my father's labourers at the gas works wearing his Sunday best, introduced himself. Heinz was his name and he was a Berliner. His accent gave him away. I couldn't believe he wanted to become an actor! He went on the same bus as I, but had to get off before me. He asked at what time I would be travelling the next morning.

'I have no idea . . . I'll likely take the *Stadtbahn*, it's faster I'm told.' I wanted to make it clear from the start - I didn't care for his company.

The next morning I was late again. My transfer bus hadn't stopped because it was full. I had been forced to wait for the next one.

Everybody looked at me when I came dashing into the dance hall. The teacher, a middle-aged lady with the body of a nymph, was lecturing to the class. The students stood around her in a semi-circle. I slipped in at one end of it. Frau Turck, who used to dance with the Berliner Ballet, was talking about minuets and gavottes and folk dances. It gave me a chance to look over my fellow students. One blonde girl right across from me caught my eye. She was the prettiest, I decided. Long, blonde hair, clear skin, and the figure of a model, but shorter. To my surprise the rest of the girls were quite ordinary looking, some you might call plain or homely. What demon gave them the guts to think people would want to see them on stage or in a film? A short fellow who looked like a plumber's assistant in his overalls was ogling me! I looked away fast. Another male student had a figure like a girl – his waist was slimmer than mine! He had a long thin torso, and he wore the tightest of tights – ugh! Next to him was a good-looking young man with ash-blond hair, who was obviously trying to catch the attention of the girl beside him. She was about my height, quite slim, and her shiny black hair flowed loosely over half of her face. Her skin was near white, and she had a chiseled Roman nose. The word ethereal came to my mind.

After our session, everyone went upstairs to the locker rooms to change. I tried to catch the attention of the ash blond fellow but he only had eyes for the ghostlike beauty. 'I'm Gerd,' I heard him say to her. 'Want to go over to Café Budapest for lunch?' Damn, he didn't even look at me – and I so wanted to get to know him! Instead I got to know the blonde beauty. She was the only one who talked to me in the locker room. Her name was Donata, and Berlin was her hometown. She had been taking dance lessons for a couple of years till somebody told her she was too tall to pursue a stage career in dance. Two girls, one with copper red hair and blue eye makeup, the other dark with short hair and a rather plain face, were giggling with each other like old friends. They were discussing an actor at the Schiller Theater who had received raving critiques as Mephistopheles in *Faust*.

'I waited at the stage entrance for him, and got his autograph,' the redhead whispered. 'Then I slipped him my telephone number. I bet he's going to call me – or I'll call him, I don't care. I want him.' Wow – I was stunned. Maybe I shouldn't give up on Gerd – make the first move myself! Show him that I'm interested in him and see what happens.

A catastrophe happened. In the coming days I tried several times to talk to him, but my heart started to thump in my chest and my breathing became so erratic, I was afraid I wouldn't be able to produce a coherent sentence. I gave up before I even opened my mouth.

I hadn't yet realized that I was a spoiled, pampered brat and so totally unsophisticated in conversation I wouldn't have been able to attract the attention of a man if I'd been the last woman on earth. It hadn't sunk in that I was a small town girl with a huge ego and a head full of dreams. I was used to my father praising me, his only daughter, and showing me off at special events in town. The fact that my teachers had acknowledged my acting ability, and that I had been chosen to ride on our float at the school's 600th anniversary, had made me think that I was special. Now, suddenly, I was nobody. I felt like I had been kicked off my pedestal and thrown into a refuse bin. For the first couple of weeks I cried myself to sleep.

Donata saved me.

'Please, Annabel, will you prompt me – just these two pages . . .' She had caught me in the hall alone, dawdling, hoping Gerd might come along and talk to me. 'I'm on next with Herr Hoffer,' she added. She handed me the text. I was eager to help her. I had just read the first cue when Hoffer opened the door to the rehearsal room and called her in. After ten minutes, Donata reappeared. Her face was red and she looked like she was going to cry. She took me by the hand, pulled me upstairs and into the locker room.

'Hoffer is so rude,' she hissed. 'Because I got stuck in my text, he dismissed me. Come back when you know your lines,' he said, 'I'm not here to prompt you.'

'Never mind him, Donata. The old sod only wants to work with Helga. He spends more time with her on her Rosalind than with all of his other students combined. I saw them in the hall today, holding hands . . . and did you notice? She no longer wears lipstick. The old goat doesn't like makeup on her, she's told me.' I was eager to console Donata.

'It's pathetic, he could be her grandfather! He's certainly past his prime, personally and professionally.' Donata was gearing up again. 'I haven't seen him in a major role in ages. I guess the adoration of a young girl pleases his ego, pompous old ass!'

'Don't worry, he's shown no interest in working with me either. He lets me go on uninterrupted and when I'm finished he says, 'You are not into it . . . it needs more study.'

Suddenly, as if she had overheard our conversation, Helga burst into the room.

'Will one of you prompt me, please? Hoffer wants to do the garden scene with me, and Elke has already left.' Elke, her bosom friend, who was trying to get Mephistopheles into bed. Likely she was off pursuing her goal.

'Sorry Helga, we have to leave. We have a very important appointment.' Donata took me by the arm.

'Very important,' I dared to shout as we dashed out of the locker room.

'Let's go to my place. We can talk undisturbed there.' Donata pulled me down the stairs and out the front door.

We took a streetcar to her apartment building. For the first time I got to see the inner city and the famous Kurfürstendamm. The stores, the cars, the people, the lovely outdoor cafés – I hadn't expected anything like it. The women were dressed in expensive, beautiful clothes; the cars were either Mercedes models or BMWs. The traffic of people and cars was rolling along in an unbroken line. One day I'll be riding in one of those cars – a convertible. I'll park in front of the most exclusive café and a handsome man who has been waiting for me, will get up and lead me to his table. The people around us will look at us and whisper, and a young girl will beg me for my autograph. I will graciously remove my sunglasses and smile at her while I write my name on her napkin. Annabel, yes, just Annabel.

Donata's family lived in a classy city apartment. The ceilings were high and curved, like in a palace, and there was intricate plaster work all around them. My eyes picked out places where big chunks of plaster were missing, and I couldn't avoid noticing long cracks in the ceiling.

'My father says one of these days the whole place will collapse on us, there is so much damage from the air raids, but Mama thinks we are lucky the building is still standing and we haven't lost our belongings, like most Berliners.' Donata opened the door to her room. We sat down on her bed and she told me about Berlin – how it had risen out of the ashes like the proverbial phoenix, and how people tried to make up for years of suffering by indulging in what a capitalist society had to offer.

'There is a lot we have to make up for, my mother often says. I think she means making love. My dad was away all through the war. I hardly remember him from when I was a child. But they have found each other again. At times it's hard to bear their turtledove behaviour.'

Towards the end of our first semester, the male students started a game: Guess who, among the first year female students, was still a virgin, who had slept with one man, and who had a lot of sexual experience. The second-year students, who generally didn't mix with us, joined in the game because of their advanced psychological knowledge.

Gerd, who to my regret hadn't ever engaged me in a conversation, stopped me in the hall. 'Annabel . . . bella Annabel, how can you express Margaret's feelings? She gives herself to Faust, and swoons with desire for him afterwards.'

I had noticed him in the rehearsal room while I was working with Hoffer on the scene at the spinning wheel. 'No wonder Hoffer wasn't satisfied with your work. Annabel, you need sexual experience, you need to have felt desire, passion, or your Margaret will never come to life'.

'How do you know I haven't had experience, hm? I don't have to advertise my personal life like Elke. I wouldn't be surprised if she's slept with half of the actors at the Schiller Theater, the way she talks. Do you think that makes her a talented actress?' I stopped my babbling. By defending myself, I had confirmed my virginity – damn!

'I'm ready to help you improve your performance, Annabella. Think of it that way, hm?' Gerd grinned. 'Unfortunately I'm taken tonight – but any other day . . .' he winked at me and was off.

Shit, damn, I hate you! No, that wasn't true. I really liked him. He wasn't only good-looking, but upbeat, intelligent and charming. What a shame he didn't care for me other than for bed. He was courting the ethereal beauty with the flowing black hair. He was continually after her, reading for her, rehearsing with her, inviting her out to lunch – his heart was with her, it couldn't have been more obvious. No, no, no, I will not lie down for him! Never mind how much I want him – or how lonely I feel.

Chapter 4

Donata, who had an on again off again boyfriend, had arranged a date for me.

'I'm sorry, Annabel, but I have to agree with Gerd. You need some experience. You are twenty years old, and as you don't want to marry, what are you saving yourself for? By the way, today's men don't expect their prospective wives to be virgins. The war has changed all that. How many girls waited faithfully for the return of their boyfriends or their fiancés – their would-be husbands. They waited for men who never came back. And now there is such a shortage of middle-aged men. We are in luck! The men of our generation were too young to be drafted. We've got a sufficient supply. Annabel, you need to go for it.'

Donata took immediate action. It happened that she had just made up with Heiko, and she enticed him to arrange a date for me with one of his friends.

'The fellow comes from a good family,' she told me. He's in his third year of studies at the Free University. Let's all meet on Sunday at the Wannsee Boat Club. I'll introduce you, and Volker, that's his name, can take you sailing. Heiko and I will go for a row. If you like him, we can go on double dates in future. Both of these guys have money, you know.'

'Alright,' I sighed. 'Why not? Anything is better than sitting in the flat alone, while Oma is out having fun with her man. How ironic! My father insisted I board with her to have supervision. Turns out I'm stuck at home on Saturday nights, while she is living it up somewhere in the city. Her friend has a car, and to add insult to injury he apologized to me last time he picked her up. He told me he was sorry that he had to leave me behind, because three, as everybody knows, is a crowd. You should have seen the grin on his face! I could have punched him. Really, my grandmother's love life bothers me! She's supposed to be past that.'

Volker passed the first-impression test. He was neither ugly nor handsome – not quite a fairy tale prince. But he had good manners and a horse – I mean he owned a pretty little sailboat. We met him on the dock at the boat club. After brief introductions, my eyes took in the vast expanse of water before me. I hadn't expected the Wannsee to be that large and to lie within the Western Zone. What a lovely spot to get away from the hustle and bustle of the city and enjoy the natural world. The sun was shining, the air was pleasantly warm, and boats of all kinds dotted the water. I couldn't imagine a more enchanting environment for my first date. I was looking forward to an exciting time. I promised myself I would give Volker a chance.

The boat lay tied up at the dock, ready to take us away. Volker jumped in and extended an arm to me while he kept the boat steady by holding onto the dock. He was wearing white running shorts and a white polo shirt that showed off his tan. I shouted, 'See you later!' to Donata and Heiko, and we were off.

As soon as we were away from shore, Volker let out the sail, and we drifted along under a mild wind – lovely. I felt that my life had reached a new stage - that I was no longer on the outside looking in but on the inside, looking out at what the world had to offer. I smiled at Volker. We sat facing each other.

'What do you think of Berlin? Have you been to the Brecht Theater in the Eastern Sector?' Volker jumped right into a subject relevant to my schooling – how thoughtful.

'No, not yet, but I hope . . .' What was that? I tried to keep my eyes on his face, though they persisted in slipping down to his shorts. Something was showing between the inside of his left thigh and his shorts – something roundish and grey. 'I'll . . . get a chance . . . to go soon,' I managed to finish my sentence. Volker moved as he adjusted the sail – maybe that thing would disappear? No, it wobbled and became even more exposed! Oh my good fairy! It's his balls - his balls were hanging out!

My date continued to chat – untroubled by my dead silence. I focussed my eyes on the bubbly trail that followed our boat. Don't look – just don't look at it! But how could I not look at him when he asked me a question? My eyes seemed to slide down on their own accord. I felt like jumping overboard – anything to get away from him!

I breathed a sigh of relief when the wind suddenly picked up and Volker suggested we turn back to the dock. 'I'm a good weather sailor,' he joked, 'not very brave.' He kept talking to me, but my mind was fixed on the grey mass, hanging there, wobbling with the slightest move he made. I said a prayer of thanks when we reached the dock and he stood up.

'Shall we go for a beer,' he suggested, 'at the club house?'

'Oh no,' I blurted out with more emphasis than I had intended. 'I have to get home to my studies. There is a test tomorrow,' I lied.

'May I call you . . . sometime . . .'

'Sure . . . that would be nice . . .' Another lie escaped my mouth. I was sure of only one thing – I never wanted to see him again!

Donata couldn't understand why I felt so hostile towards him. I had been too embarrassed to tell her the truth about his balls. I wasn't totally ignorant – I had seen male genitals. Our neighbours' two little boys often ran around naked in the summer. Their firm little balls looked cute. And I had seen pictures of Michelangelo's David and reproductions of other classical Roman heroes in the nude. Their balls had not offended me. Maybe the artists didn't want to frighten young virgins. They had kept the balls firmly attached to the body and of moderate size. No wobbling there! Did all men look like Volker? Were male genitals really that ugly? That night, to get the image of Volker's balls out of my mind, I lay down on my bed and picked up *Gone with the Wind* by Margaret Mitchell. I had seen the movie and had walked out of the theatre in a dream-like state, blind to reality. Scarlett and Butler's love was passionate and wild, and sooo romantic. I read till two o'clock in the morning and fell asleep in Clark Gable's arms. When he made love to me in my dream nothing ugly, nothing wobbly spoiled my pleasure.

Chapter 5

Donata's love relationship was off again – she had found Heiko wanting – in fidelity. And though she didn't quite understand my dislike towards Volker, she accepted my excuse. He wasn't my type. To console ourselves and to get some exposure, she came up with a brilliant idea. 'The Arts Club is sponsoring a dance. Let's go! The club's social affairs are legendary for the people you can meet there: painters, sculptors, well-known actors and models, fashion and others. We are bound to connect with attractive males.' Though tickets were hard to come by, Donata managed. She had connections. I imagined one of the up and coming Berlin painters falling in love with me, and asking me to model for him. I saw myself spread out on a divan like Goya's *Naked Maja* and my lover, wearing an artist's tunic and dark locks down to his shoulders, labouring behind the canvas. From time to time he would drop his brush and dash up to me to press a hot kiss on my lips. Yes, I was ready to go to the artists' ball.

What to wear? I owned nothing fashionable for such an occasion. I bought a blouse, semi-low cut, at *Wertheim's*. The famous department store had been re-opened and was once again favoured by an international clientele. At *KaDeWe* a similar blouse would have cost me half of what I paid – never mind, I was determined to make an impression. Instead of buying the odd knackwurst with a bun from the vendor at the corner, I would dig more heartily into the free fare the Amis were providing at the school. Maybe I could fast on Lung Stew Day – there was one without fail every week – it was said to sharpen your senses, fasting.

As we entered the club, I noticed only couples sitting around the tables. Before I had a chance to regret the amount of money I had spent on my blouse, Donata pulled me into the centre of the room – she had spotted two empty chairs. I looked around. The walls were covered with – art? I guessed that's what it was supposed to be. These wild splashes of colour and horrid scenes of wounded cut-up bodies didn't enhance the surroundings. Fortunately the lights were low – and the candles on the tables made for a more pleasant atmosphere. And so did the people. They were chatting, laughing, making as much noise as school kids at recess time. 'Do they all know each other,' I asked Donata, 'They are so – informal, so merry and . . .'

'Would you like to dance?' A well-dressed young man, who had been sitting at a table near us, bowed at my side. He had left behind a most gorgeous young woman whom Donata had recognized as one of Berlin's top models.

I was stunned. Why me? I felt like I was Cinderella at the ball, and the prince had just asked me for a dance. And it wasn't only one dance I enjoyed with him. Robert, that was his name, asked me again and again. In between he danced with the beauty at his table. He wasn't a great dancer, but we managed to shuffle along with only an occasional collision of our feet. Donata said we made an attractive pair – the fashion model was too tall for him. When the music stopped and the party was breaking up, he came rushing towards me.

'I would like to see you again, Annabel – may I?'

'But what about your girlfriend?' I blurted out.

'She'll be alright. I'd like to get to know you, sweet Annabel.'

Oh my good fairy! Is it true? Has the prince chosen *me*? I gave Robert my phone number. I hoped Oma wouldn't answer the phone and maybe invite him over, because Robert came from a good family. His father, who had been a lawyer in Hanover, had fallen in the last year of the war, and now his son was studying at the *Freie Universität,* retracing his dad's footsteps. 'I can get a job in my father's old firm soon as I'm finished,' he had told me. I had felt the need to brag about my father: his intelligence, his wit, his important job as director of the gas works. I liked talking about him – it made me feel as though he wasn't so far away.

Robert and I met again one day in the city, after school. He bought me a carafe of coffee and encouraged me to have a cream puff, my favourite pastry. Was my dream starting to become reality? Here I was, sitting in one of the outdoor cafés on Kurfürstendamm, the waiter was pouring my coffee, and Robert was asking me if the pastry was to my liking. I sat back in my chair and watched well-dressed people pass by. So far, all the eating out I had been able to afford was a piece of *Blutwurst* with a bun at *Fachinger's*, the favourite eatery for starving students and street bums. Now, here I was – in a first class establishment! Once the sun had set, Robert paid the bill and walked me to my bus stop. He invited me to join him at the next meeting of his drama club.

'We read and discuss new plays. You, as a drama student, would be more than welcome, Annabel.' Robert must have noticed my insecurity – he added, 'We are all amateurs . . . you have nothing to fear. Please come – we meet at my place next Wednesday.'

I was late as usual. I had taken the *Stadtbahn,* as Robert had suggested, but got lost on my way to his house. I was exhausted when I entered his lodgings. I had been running around in circles for twenty minutes. An animated discussion was in full swing. Nobody noticed me in the haze of smoke that filled the room. People were slouching on the sofa bed, on the floor, on some orange crates. For a moment I was ready to sneak out, run away. But Robert saw me, took me by the hand and introduced me like I was the long-awaited star of the gathering.

The play to be read and discussed was *Six People Are Looking For An Author* by Pirandello, a new Italian playwright. It was a complicated piece of work. I understood very little, but I read the part of a young woman as if I knew what it was all about.

When his friends started to leave, Robert asked me to stay for a few more minutes. I told him I was worried about getting home, late, in the dark.

'I'll walk you to the *Stadtbahn*. The last one runs at twelve thirty. My landlady doesn't allow visitors after midnight anyway. You've got plenty of time.' The landlady's rule reassured me. She would be close and keep watch.

I didn't mind staying. Robert's room was cozy. It was lit by a couple of candles that flickered on the table. He poured two glasses of wine, and we sat down, side by side, on his sofa bed. Even in the dim light I couldn't help noticing that he wasn't a handsome man. His nose was too long, and his eyes were too close together. I couldn't help thinking of Laurence Olivier whom I had seen for the first time in *Hamlet*. I had dreamed of him night after night. Robert took my hand and brought me back to reality. He gently played with my fingers while we talked – about the play, about our studies, about our families.

'Your future husband will have a hard time competing with your father,' Robert joked. I must have bragged about my Papa again. He pulled me closer and kissed me – a long kiss – first gently and then more thoroughly. He knew how to do it. He certainly had acquired the skill. It felt – exhilarating. I kissed him back. Robert slid down on his back and pulled me on top of him.

'I don't want to have sex, not yet, promise . . .' I mumbled. Our closeness felt - exciting. Robert kept holding me tight. He kept kissing me. He ran his tongue around my lips - oh what a sensation! It made me feel hot and strangely agitated, but I didn't want him to stop. 'Promise you won't do it . . . even if I don't resist . . .' I needed his reassurance - I couldn't trust myself any more.

'Promise,' he said.

He kept kissing my neck, behind my ears, my earlobes. One of his legs had ended up between my thighs, but I didn't feel like pushing it away. An electric current was running through me – getting stronger and stronger – I felt my heart thumping against Robert's chest . . . I could hardly breathe . . .

'You're sure you don't want to . . .?' Robert's muffled voice.

'I'm sure,' I panted, 'yes please . . . not . . . I'm sure . . .' I forced my eyes to open and sat up. My hair had tumbled into my face. I felt drops of sweat on my forehead. I brushed my hair back and looked at Robert. His shirt was all crumpled up and his tie . . .

'Oh no,' I screamed, 'look at your tie . . .'

Robert pulled the loosely hanging piece of cloth over his head. He held it towards the candlelight. It looked like a rabid cat had got hold of it.

'You've chewed up my tie,' he laughed. 'How passionate you are, Annabella.'

As promised, Robert walked me to the *Stadtbahn* station. I arrived safely home with my body intact and my mind in utter bewilderment.

Poor Robert – when he came to visit me at Oma's unannounced, I was furious. As I had feared, my darling grandmother had answered his telephone call, and had invited him over. She was eager to get me hooked up – maybe she wanted me out of her flat on weekends. I hadn't been sure I wanted to see Robert again – I couldn't ask him to be 'understanding' a second time, and I didn't want him to see my grandmother's modest little flat. I left him standing at the door, grabbed my coat and pulled him down the stairs.

'Let's walk to the lake . . . I need fresh air. I've been studying all afternoon – we have end of semester exams tomorrow.' That was the truth. What I didn't tell him was that I had long neglected my studies because I had spent hours at the Arts Cinema. The theatre had been presenting a Laurence Olivier Week, showing all of his films. I had watched *Lady Hamilton, Wuthering Heights, Pride and Prejudice, Richard the Fifth, Rebecca,* and *Hamlet* – again. I was totally and hopelessly in love with Olivier. I even contemplated a visit to the Pinewood Studios in London. Luckily I didn't have the required finances. It saved me from making a fool of myself.

Poor Robert – I was horrible company. In the bright daylight I noticed that he really wasn't handsome – that long nose, and those squashy little eyes . . . He had brought me a bunch of violets, a sweet little bouquet tied with a blue ribbon. While we walked I kept twisting it around in my hand till it finally fell to the ground. Robert picked it up and handed it to me. He kissed my hand.

'I'm sorry Robert, but I really need to get back,' I mumbled. 'I have to study. I'm worried about tomorrow – you understand?'

I was telling the truth. I was worried. I had wasted so much time with my extracurricular activities. I was ill prepared for the exams. How could I let this happen? My dream would never come true if I didn't buckle down! Never mind the drama coaches giving me little of their time and little encouragement. It was up to me to make myself visible – attract their attention! 'Flirt with them,' Oma had advised me. 'They are men, aren't they?' That seemed to be a sensible solution - why hadn't I done it? I didn't feel attracted to them - that's why. If one of them had been like Olivier . . . oh yes . . . that would've made for a different story.

My brief story with Robert ended when he left Berlin for the holidays. We had talked on the phone a couple of times, and I hadn't encouraged him to look me up on his return. Our paths never crossed again. But in my memory he'll always be the example of a true gentleman.

Chapter 6

My darling Papa had sent me the money to fly home for the summer holidays. He knew I wasn't keen on riding the train through the *Deutsche Demokratische Republik* again – and having my underwear exposed to my fellow travellers. Not that I had replaced the seductive negligée. Oma would have had an attack of hysteric laughter had she seen me flaunting it in our modest flat. It just didn't go with the smell of cigarette smoke and fried onions that permanently inhabited each nook and cranny of the place.

The Tempelhof Airport was as busy as it had been during the Blockade in the summer of 1948, when the Soviets had closed the Eastern Zone to all ground traffic. Now people preferred to fly for convenience sake – or because their name was in the black book. They didn't want to run the risk of being arrested and imprisoned by the Stasi, the secret police.

There are no borders in the air, and the sky goes on forever and ever, I discovered. It was my first flight and a feeling of exhilaration took hold of me. Never mind the teachers and students ignoring me at school – I would show them! My time would come! My career would take off like our plane, and rise, rise up to the sun!

My dreams of greatness were forgotten when I met my Papa at Hanover Airport. To be held in his arms, to hear his voice, to look into his eyes made me feel whole. How easy it was to be his little girl again, to bask in the security of his affection. Why did I need so much more? Why? Papa's face had lit up when he spotted me. But there was one more reason for his happiness. He had been featured in the town's weekly rag, picture and all, as a hero. He had managed single-handedly to stop a leak in a major pipe that could have blown up the entire gas works and damaged the houses in the neighbourhood. He was celebrated and appreciated by the community – he was the man most talked about in town. I was happy for him. I knew how he loved all that attention.

One of my former classmates, who had never gone away to university and was now working in his father's plumbing business, invited me to a dance at the Rowing Club. The atmosphere in the hall was cold and restrained when we arrived. Only after the male attendants had downed a good number of beers, did it warm up. Several boys asked me for a dance. Their legs were stiff, but their arms were strong. They squeezed me like a lemon. They must have been kayakers. Their conversation revolved around our little town, their boat races, and their drinking habits. The girls, most of them I knew, had the same hairstyles they had worn in school. The baker's daughter still had two braided rolls over her ears; she wore a dirndl and flat shoes, which made her look like one of those Austrian dolls people bring home from their holidays. A girl I had sat in class with for six years, and had hardly ever spoken to, asked me for advice on dating. She was in a panic – most girls from our class were married or engaged by now. I told her not to worry. One could enjoy the company of men without marrying them.

'Is that what you are doing in Berlin?' she whispered.

'I certainly am,' I answered. When I saw the colour rising in her face, and shock widening her pupils, I added, 'but I don't sleep with them.'

'How do you manage that, Anna?' Her look of shock had turned to admiration.

'It's a skill you acquire in the big city – naturally you have to be able to get around – and there are many handsome boys in the school, and we have dances. Some of the popular actors from the Schiller Theater will join us – you might even find two or three film stars. Oh, there is plenty of opportunity to meet attractive men.' My schoolmate heaved a sigh, and I was granted another adoring look. I felt sorry for her – and for myself.

I was more than ready to leave when my partner finally took me home. We stood in silence at my front door. Then, without warning, he lunged forward with the intention to kiss me. He missed the mark. We bumped noses and his kiss ended up on my cheek. Obviously he lacked experience. Embarrassing to be kissed on the cheek at my age! I couldn't wait to be back in the city and work on my dream.

My stepmama, the gossip she was, told me what had happened to some of my other classmates.

'Ursel is married, you know . . . and she has a baby, a little boy. I met her at the store the other day. Is he ever cute . . . and Monica is getting a divorce, would you believe it? Married only two years and giving up.'

I mumbled something like I could have told her so. We had consumed a few glasses of wine and Mama was on a roll. She dared to ask me the question that occupied her mind.

'How about you, Anna . . . are you seeing a boy in Berlin . . . have you found a nice friend?' Oh my good fairy, she was so inhibited! What she wanted to know was: Are you still a virgin? No, I'm no longer a virgin, I wanted to scream – just to shock her. I decided otherwise. She couldn't help being such a timid mouse.

'No Mama, I haven't found a boyfriend – I'm too busy with my studies,' I lied. No sense in telling her about my catastrophic encounters. She wouldn't know how to interpret them – and neither did I.

For the last week of my holidays my darling Papa took me to Norderney, the most fashionable one of the North Sea islands. We had been dining in an elegant restaurant when a beauty contest, sponsored by the most popular champagne producer, was announced. To please my Papa, I agreed to take part. I swayed along the catwalk imitating Brigitte Bardot while hugging a huge champagne bottle to my breast. I won! I was crowned *Miss Henkell Trocken* and presented with a case of champagne - a small case. People were clapping, flashbulbs were flashing, a crown was placed on my head. My darling Papa was so proud of me! He believed in me! The promise of fame and fortune seemed within reach. When the band started to play dance music, some men, wealthy according to my Papa, asked me for a dance - one dance. None came back for a second time. Did they sense my naiveté, my unsophistication, my sexual innocence? I made up my mind right there and then: I would have a sexual experience - I would become some man's lover - and if it killed me!

Chapter 7

After promising my father I wouldn't let my success as Champagne Queen swell my head, and reassuring my stepmother that I wouldn't get involved with unworthy men of dubious reputation, I was back on the plane heading for Berlin. I couldn't help noticing that the man in the seat beside me wore an expensive suit and Italian-made shoes. I studied his profile – very distinguished, middle age, greying temples. He was reading a newspaper and I noticed a wedding ring flashing among his suntanned fingers. I gambled on his being tired of the drudgery of married life, and ready for a bit on the side, as Oma called it. How to get his attention? He was deeply buried in the newspaper, studying columns of numbers.

'Do you fly often?' I asked – my voice sounding higher than usual.

He dropped the paper, gave me a look like I had just fallen out of the sky and mumbled, 'Always.'

I feverishly tried to figure out a more effective approach. The stewardess was serving drinks. He opted for Coca Cola. I asked for the same. Then I remembered a French movie. The great courtesan Madame du Barry had dropped her handkerchief to attract the attention of a handsome nobleman at the court of Louis XV. I rummaged first in my pockets, then in my handbag for a clean hanky – and knocked over my glass of cola. It landed in the lap of my neighbour and emptied its content all down his leg. He jumped up, the paper sailed to the floor, and the colour in his face turned frighteningly red.

'You clumsy child,' he grumbled. In seconds the stewardess was at his side, sponging his leg with a damp cloth. They both looked at me like I had just set the plane on fire. I mumbled several apologies but was ignored. The attendant guided the man to another seat, well away from me. Behind me an old lady kept clucking away about the bad manners of young people nowadays. I crawled into myself, closed my eyes, and imagined the man and the stewardess being sucked out of the plane by a sudden explosion, and dumped into space where they had to whirl around weightlessly forever and ever.

Oma picked up on my low mood when I got back to her flat.

'What happened, Anna, did my daughter give you a hard time? Did she question your morals? She has such a limited outlook on life, love and sex. I certainly don't know where that comes from.'

'Oh no, I can handle her . . . but . . .' I told her what had happened on the plane. I skipped over the handkerchief episode - just told her about the spilled cola.

'That stuff is sticky, you know. He'll remember you for a long time! Oh, cheer up darling, you'll never see him again, the old sourpuss. I have been thinking while you were away . . . it's not right for you to be cooped up here every weekend . . . going to movies as your only entertainment, dreaming of celluloid men! You need to get out - meet the real thing, be where the action is. I'll write to your father about getting you a room in the city, close to your friend Donata, so you can have a social life . . . go for dances . . . meet a nice fellow . . . Anna, would you like to live downtown on your own?'

Would I like it? The idea was so exciting it made me forget the incident on the plane. I imagined myself in my own cozy room, entertaining some young people of class, arranging poetry readings and musical soirées.

'Yes Oma,' I shouted, 'please write to Papa. If the idea comes from you he won't object.' It occurred to me that Oma's concern about my social life wasn't completely unselfish. She wanted her flat back – for you know what.

My darling Papa agreed with Oma's suggestion and sent, by return mail, the first month's rent for my room. I started my search with great enthusiasm – only to find out that accommodation in Berlin was sparse. There were many buildings as yet under construction, and many blocks were still in ruins. When I talked about my unsuccessful search in school, Gerd, who had offered to free me of the burden of virginity, made me another offer. He had to go home to Düsseldorf for a week or two, on a personal matter, and I was welcome to occupy his space.

'But remember, Annabel, only to the end of the month – unless you want to spend a few nights in my bed with me.' He smiled his irresistible smile and scribbled down his address.

Gerd's room was only a block away from the famous *Gedächtniskirche*, the Kaiser-Wilhelm-Memorial Church, which was kept intact, or rather in ruins, as a reminder of the destructive forces of war. His landlady, a war widow, asked me into her parlour for coffee the very first day, and offered me the use of her kitchen. That helped. Oma had been good enough to supply me with food, now I had to fend for myself. It didn't take me long to learn to cook spaghetti and to open a tin of tomato sauce – and, if my budget allowed, to fry some ground beef for a meat sauce. A feeling of glorious freedom made my heart sing.

At night, when I snuggled down in Gerd's bed, I couldn't help dreaming about him. How would it feel if he lay beside me? Why did he have to fall for the esoteric beauty? Donata and I had our doubts about her feelings towards him. She played it cool – did that make him chase her so ardently?

It felt weird and exciting to live among his things. I had to satisfy my curiosity by checking out each item in the room. In the first couple of days I went through every drawer and read every letter he had received. I discovered that he had a girlfriend in Düsseldorf – there was a whole bunch of letters from her. The latest explained his 'personal matter'. She was pregnant! She had tried strenuous physical exercise, and had sat in a scalding bath for hours while downing a number of hot toddies. It hadn't worked. She urged him to come immediately – she couldn't trust herself – she was afraid of what she might do! Wow! Lighthearted, charming Gerd! What would he do?

Another party was announced at school. *A Midsummer Night's Dream* was the theme, but as usual, any kind of fantastic dress was accepted. Gerd's landlady helped my transformation. She suggested I wear my leotards. 'You have such a lovely bottom,' was her comment. She fished around in her drawers and produced a couple of colourful shawls. She draped them with artistic flair around my hips and over my shoulders.

'My husband sent these shawls from France. He was stationed there for a while. He was such a thoughtful man.'

She smiled a far-away smile. Then she jumped to her feet.

'This is no time for sentimental memories, Annabel. Now it's your turn! You go out there and dazzle them. You look . . . enticing.'

I was excited because I wouldn't have to leave the party early to catch the last train to Tegel. In the city, the streetcars ran till two in the morning on Saturdays. Lots of time for dancing and getting drunk – on Coca Cola. No alcoholic drinks allowed. And I didn't need them. I got intoxicated by the music, the dancing, and by the wild, unrestrained atmosphere of the place. Most of the male teachers attended, together with students from the Arts Club and young actors from the Schiller Theater.

Some of the guests disappeared at intervals into the darkness of the garden with one or the other drama student, to return, after a short time, in high spirits. They are taking 'a substance' Donata whispered in my ear. Wine? Beer? I had no idea what she meant.

It didn't bother me that only the boys I wasn't keen on asked me to dance. I just wanted to be on the floor, in the middle of the crowd, moving, twirling, jumping about like the creatures of the forest in Shakespeare's *Midsummer Night's Dream*. I didn't need a 'substance'; I was turned on from inside myself.

After midnight the music became softer; candles were lit on windowsills, and only couples kept dancing, clinging tightly to each other, unaware of their surroundings. Heinz, the working-class boy, hadn't given up on me over all the months. I had danced a couple of times with him, unable to refuse because nobody else was asking. Now he was heading my way again. I darted over to Donata and pulled her outside. The wide marble staircase was littered with snogging couples. We had to thread our way with care down to the lawn.

'Hello Annabel, I have been looking for you - come dance with me.' Jürgen, the fellow of the small waist and tight tights, pulled me back into the house. He held me close. It was easy to follow his steps this way.

I was delighted how well we danced together – delighted to be part of a couple enjoying the last dance.

'I've been wanting to hold you close for a long time, Annabel,' he whispered, 'but you never even look my way . . . don't you like me?'

The tight leotards, hmm . . .

'I like you,' I answered, and it was the truth. At that moment I did.

'Come,' he said, 'let's have another cola and talk.'

We did. I knew he was intelligent, but I hadn't known that he had studied theatre for two years at university, and that his ambition was to direct plays – or films. He criticized the old geezer for the way he worked with me – or didn't work, spending most of his time trying to make an actress out of his adored Helga.

'The man has nothing to give – he's burned out. He's trying to re-kindle his fire by shagging a young girl – disgusting.'

I couldn't have agreed with him more.

'I'm leaving, Annabel, this kind young man here is giving me a ride.' Donata, looking hot and happy, had found me. 'Are you alright getting home?'

'I'll take her,' Jürgen took my hand. 'Good night, farewell Donata.'

The party was over. Only a few die-hards were still talking on the outdoor staircase.

'What time is it,' I asked Jürgen. 'I hope I didn't miss my last streetcar.'

'You have . . . I'm glad. I'd like you to come to my place for a glass of wine . . . we can walk.'

I knew drinking wine wasn't the only thing on his mind, but I didn't care. He was much nicer than I had expected, and I enjoyed talking to him. So he had a slim waist and a long torso . . . nobody was perfect, including myself.

The wine helped to get me into his bed.

'We'll just lie here, Annabel, and I'll hold you. Doesn't that feel good?'

It did – it felt very good.

Then Jürgen kissed me on my mouth, on my neck, my breasts. That felt good too. I knew what would happen, and I was ready for it – in my head.

'Make sure I don't get pregnant,' I mumbled while he rolled down my leotards, slowly and with care. I was glad I remembered my brother's advice.

'I'll make absolutely sure,' he mumbled back.

I allowed Jürgen to proceed. But he couldn't. Not because of any defect on his part, oh no, there was indeed something big and hard poking at me – only it had no place to go! I wasn't sure where the thing was supposed to enter; my carnal knowledge was limited to some disgusting drawings in public washrooms. But in it should go – of that I was sure.

'Open your legs, Annabel, and relax. I won't hurt you, I promise.'

Jürgen was patient and loving. He kissed me, my neck, my breasts – I opened my legs, closed my eyes, and took a deep breath. I can do this – I can . . . ouch – it hurt. I was clamped up again, clamped tight like an oyster. There was no way Jürgen could get in.

After a third attempt, he gave up. He went to the bathroom.

'Let's go to sleep,' he said when he came back – not unkindly.

I couldn't sleep. Jürgen had dropped off with his arms around me. I didn't dare move. I was afraid he might wake up and the whole horror show might start again. The light of dawn was looking in at the window when finally I dozed off.

Jürgen was very good about the unsuccessful event. It was Sunday and he took me to an outdoor café in Grunewald. He bought me a *Berliner Weisse*, the pink beer speciality, served in a huge bowl-shaped glass, my first. We talked about our classes, about the little help we got from the teachers, our chances for finding employment in a profession over-crowded with idealistic hopefuls. Neither of us mentioned the catastrophic event of the previous night. Some young couples, obviously in love, were sharing the tables around us. I was pleased to have Jürgen at my side. I'm sure we looked like any other regular couple. Nobody could have guessed my virginity.

Monday in school, I didn't know how to behave towards him. I wanted him to know I wasn't after him. I played it like nothing had happened between us. I copied the behaviour of the esoteric beauty towards Gerd – I was as cool as the Snow Queen. It worked. He never said another intimate word to me – what a pity!

Chapter 8

I had a breakthrough, finally, with Juliet. The director of the school, who was nicknamed Madame X, had praised me. She didn't use the rehearsal hall but conducted her classes in her private office, which, with its wood-panelled walls, the thick carpet, and the elegant antique furniture, felt more like a living room. Her appearance matched the environment. She was a beautiful woman, always well dressed and made up. Her snow-white hair fell to just below the ear in soft waves, and her blue eyes looked enormous behind her thick glasses. A subtle scent of lavender surrounded her. In her heydays she had been a celebrated film actress, and she had managed to preserve her flair. I imagined myself emanating that same mysterious aura when I reached her age.

My emotional performance, we had worked on the balcony scene, had a grounding in reality. I was in love, truly in love! My prince was called Daniel, and he was a new student. Because he had taken drama training with a private coach, he was admitted to our second-year class.

Madame X herself had asked him to read Romeo for me. He was only slightly taller than I, had dark hair that fell over his forehead in a short bang, and the deepest, darkest brown eyes I had ever looked into. He was charming in an unselfconscious, innocent way. Every girl in our class wanted to help him – love him.

It had been easy to love Laurence Olivier – he was far away and unobtainable. To love Daniel, whom I met every day in school, was a heartache. And to watch Bruna, who had been voted 'sexually most experienced,' dig her claws into him, was agony. The greedy bitch! She had a long-time relationship with an older man in her hometown, Hamburg. He frequently sent her airplane tickets for weekend visits. Once, when her classes didn't allow her to fly to him, she had tried to make friends with Donata and me. To get close to us, she had confessed her whole sordid love life, hoping to make an impression.

'I'm not only acting here,' she had hissed. 'I have to perform for him as well. One day he wanted me to be a waitress, and he insisted I wear nothing but a little white apron, the lecherous beast,' she had giggled.

Donata and I had been disgusted. My poor, sweet, innocent Romeo – she would devour him!

One afternoon I waited for him in the hall. I had planned to ask him to read Romeo for me again, in the bedroom scene, but I lost my courage at the last second and let him escape through the front door. Before I could go into emotional meltdown the door opened up again, and he stood before me.

'Annabel, I was going to ask you . . . I'd like to study Romeo properly, not just read for you. Will you rehearse with me?'

Hallelujah! I heard the heavens opening up above me, as a choir of angels was singing my praises!

Hold it . . . breathe out . . . don't show your eagerness.

'If you like, sure,' I said in what I thought was my normal voice – just an octave higher.

'Thank you, great. How about tomorrow?' His dark brown eyes were looking deep into my own. I detected a weakness in my knees. I nodded. I was afraid he would discover my excitement if I opened my mouth again.

'Till tomorrow then,' he called over his shoulder as he walked out the door a second time.

I stood alone in the hall, dazed. I tested my legs – they moved. Better get out fast before someone entered and noticed my state of rapture. I pirouetted towards the exit and bumped into the bust of Goethe standing watch by the door. I threw my arms around his wise head and placed a kiss on his marble mouth.

I was glad Gerd hadn't kicked me out yet. His 'private affair' took longer than he had planned. Daniel and I could study in his room.

It was just the two of us, the next night, after school. The landlady, when she met us in the hall, gave me a knowing smile. It meant she wouldn't disturb us. I deposited Daniel on Gerd's sofa bed and darted across the hall into the kitchen. The water had never run through the coffee filter so slowly! I scooted back into the room. Daniel was walking about, rehearsing his lines, mumbling to himself.

'Coffee is coming . . . won't be long,' I shouted.

In the kitchen I put cups, sugar and milk on a tray and carried it into my room.

'Coffee is ready,' I sang.

Daniel sat down on the only comfortable chair in the room. I placed the tray on a small tea table beside him. It was more intimate than the large dining table. I knelt down on the floor. We drank our coffee in silence. I avoided looking at him. I thought better let him start the conversation – I didn't want to sound eager. Daniel emptied his cup, looked around the room, swished the cloth off the dining table, wrapped it around my waist, and tucked it in at the front. I hardly dared to breathe. I felt the warmth of his body – a strange new scent floated into my nostrils – my heart began to flutter.

'Now climb onto the table, that's your balcony, and we'll start.' He carefully lifted the cloth, stretched out his hand and helped me climb up. I felt wobbly – was it the table or my knees? Daniel grabbed his jacket, turned it inside out and with an elegant swoosh draped it around his shoulders. He messed up his hair and jumped into action.

He jests at stars that never felt a wound.-
But, soft! What light through yonder window breaks?
It is the east, and Juliet is the sun!

Daniel was singing, dragging out the words in the old-fashioned style of Edmund Kean. Was he joking? He sounded like one of the old records made by famous actors years ago. I didn't dare laugh – just in case.

Daniel sing-songed on and made the most elaborate gestures with his arms through the entire monologue.

> O, that I were a glove upon her hand, (He pretended to put on a glove, inserting each finger laborously.)
> That I might touch that cheek. (He stroked one of his cheeks in the most loving manner.)

Now it was my turn. With Juliet's sigh, Ay me! I exploded into a burst of laughter. I lost all control, the table started to wobble, it tipped to one side, I slid off and landed in a heap at Daniel's feet.

'I was wondering how long you would be able to hold on,' Daniel was choking with laughter. 'Did you really think I was serious?'

'No . . . yes, maybe . . . I don't know what your drama coach has taught you . . . hah-hah tee-hee. . .' I kept sitting on the floor, laughing like a hyena.

'And you didn't want to hurt me, Annabel!' Daniel sputtered. 'How considerate you are.'

The rehearsal was finished. Neither of us could stop laughing long enough to go on. We chatted about favouritism in school, about our parents, our hometowns. We discovered that both of us had southern blood in our veins. Daniel's mother was of Spanish heritage, and my birthmother had been French, I told him. Part French, really, but I didn't think I had to be that exact. We were both thrilled to be in a big city as alive and prosperous as Berlin. I imagined us strolling hand in hand along Kurfürstendamm, dropping into one of the many bars or taking in a cabaret show. After midnight we would cuddle up in my bed and love each other. Only problem, neither of us had any money to spare – and so far, I hadn't been very successful in making love!

When Daniel had to leave he gave me a good, tight hug at the door. I dream-walked back into my room and threw myself onto the sofa bed. His scent was still hanging in the air. Why had he hugged me? Why had he left me? Was he going to see Bruna, the man-eating dragoness? My emotions seesawed up and down. He had asked me to study with him – he had hugged me – he had left me – for whom? I got down on the carpet and practiced some body awareness exercises – a mixture of disciplines taken from oriental cultures. They were the specialty of Madame Cloutot, an eccentric, single, late-middle-aged lady. Most students didn't know what to make of her exercises, but Donata and I loved her sessions, because she paid attention to us. Now I imagined hearing her voice, 'Let yourself go, Annabel, breathe from the centre . . . all movement springs from the centre . . . lower your centre into the floor . . . breathe from the centre.' I wanted to scream from the centre: Daniel, Daniel do you love me? Do you want to make love to me? Why did you leave me . . . why?

During the next week we worked on the balcony scene with Madame X. Sheer joy! Oh could his/Romeo's words of devotion be addressed to me! We rehearsed twice in an empty classroom – just the two of us. Twice Bruna came marching in with some stupid excuse. Would Daniel please remember that he had promised to take her to the Arts Cinema that night? Would he please quiz her after we were finished rehearsing? I pretended not to care, but I was boiling! Give me a poisoned apple – or a lance, so I can pierce her heart!

It happened when we were rehearsing again in Gerd's room. Daniel had suggested the bedroom scene and I was more than willing to consent. He asked me to lie down on the bed, and with one quick leap he slumped down beside me. He wrapped his arms around me, rested his head on my shoulder and closed his eyes. My heart began to thump – oh that disturbing scent! Suddenly Daniel lifted his head, kissed me passionately, disentangled himself, jumped out of bed and stood up. Pause . . . Daniel looked at me . . . then nodded. Oh my lines!

Wilt thou be gone? It is not yet near day.
It was the nightingale and not the lark,
That pierced the fearful hollow of thine ear.

I was able to go on with my text, but I hardly dared look into his eyes. Daniel in contrast was totally into it. Several times he grabbed me, other times he held my hand – he was the wild and passionate lover Shakespeare had created. He ignored the appearance of the nurse at the end of the scene, grabbed me and muttered,

Farewell, farewell! One kiss and I'll descend.

But he didn't. He held onto me and kissed me, kissed me . . . I prayed, don't stop, please don't stop . . .

'That's not in the text,' I managed to whisper when I was able to breathe again.

'It should be,' Daniel whispered back.

We ended up under the covers. This time I was ready for it. I looked into his deep, dark eyes and melted. There was no clamping up, only, way back in my head, the fear of pregnancy. I managed to voice it.

'I'll be careful,' Daniel assured me. I trusted him. Daniel, sweet Daniel, so close, his bare skin on mine, his hand stroking me gently, and finally closer still, inside me. There was little pain, no strong physical sensation, but I was overwhelmed with emotion. Tears were trickling down my cheeks. Daniel held me close.

'You are so beautiful, so pure,' he whispered. He kissed my wet cheeks. We lay quietly, side by side, his arm around my neck. Oh, why couldn't we stay like this forever!

'I can love you again now, my Annabel,' he whispered after a while, as if he had read my thoughts. And he did.

While we were about to fall asleep, a sudden thought made me laugh out loud.

'What's funny?' Daniel asked.

'I lost my virginity in Gerd's bed,' I grinned, 'but not with him!'

'Good for me,' Daniel mumbled. I felt his body relax in my arms.

Chapter 9

Two more months! That's all the time I had left at school and my role studies weren't exactly promising. I had to do something - something. With my heart beating in my throat, and sweaty palms, I dared to approach the old geezer. He had been standing alone in the hall, likely waiting for his beloved Helga. In answer to my plea for help he told me, in the calmest of voices, that the part I had chosen, Margaret in Goethe's *Faust*, wasn't suitable for me – that's why my work was a failure.

'It's too late in the game to do something about it,' he concluded. For a second I stood there, my mouth open, my breathing suspended. My brain felt like an empty hole – like all of my dreams, my whole future had been knocked out of it. Finally, with a hollow voice, I managed to say: 'Why didn't you tell me before?'

'I was sure you would come to this conclusion yourself, Fräulein Lambert – if you had paid attention to your studies.' He donned his hat and escaped through the door.

Oh my good fairy, why didn't I speak up! Why didn't I challenge him! Once my heart had found its regular rhythm, and my brain was working again, I realized there was truth in his statement. I had spent most of my time worrying about my love life, and given little attention to my studies. After my night with Daniel my thoughts had been exclusively on him. Did he want to be with me again? Did he prefer Bruna? Why did he behave so 'neutral' towards me in school? All I could do was wait and worry. I couldn't let him know I wanted him. I was convinced that once you showed a man you loved him, he would abandon you. There was no challenge – and men needed a challenge. I had learned that from Scarlett O'Hara. All I could do was wait – and not look eager for his attention.

It paid off. Daniel asked me to go to the Arts Cinema with him on a Sunday. No suggestion of rehearsing, just a regular date. I was in heaven! After the show we went to his room. He made coffee in his landlady's kitchen, and we sat on his bed and talked. We were both awestruck by the movie we had seen, *Children of Olympus*, with the great mime Jean-Louis Barrault. Oh, to be able to act like him, to move like him! How much we had to learn, Daniel concluded. He had taken me into his arms and was about to kiss me when the doorbell rang. We heard voices in the hall, then a knock on his door.

BRUNA! My heart sank. She looked very surprised, but managed to be casual.

'Oh hello Annabel, have you two been rehearsing?' She didn't wait for an answer but looked intensely at Daniel.

'I'm just passing by . . . I thought you might want to see a film with me, Daniel. *Children of Olympus* is on at the Art Cinema, just for today. You told me you wanted to see it.'

'Annabel and I just got back from there,' Daniel answered – and my heart jumped back into its regular place. He didn't invite her to stay, but kept her standing by the door.

'Alright . . .' Bruna smiled her sweetest smile, 'I guess I'll call on Donata, she must be lonely without you Annabel. I'll see y-o-u tomorrow Daniel.' She had dragged out the *you* to give it special meaning. Then she turned and left.

Neither of us said a word about the interference. There was no more light coming in through the window. Daniel pulled the curtains shut and lit a candle. He looked into my eyes, wrapped me into his arms, kissed me long and intensively. Then, without letting go of my mouth, he undressed me, slowly, piece by piece. He shed his clothing and we cuddled up, stroking each other, basking in each other's nakedness. And finally our bodies were merging, coming together, heightening my feelings and surprising me with new sensations. It felt so much more intense than the first time. It made me forget my fear of pregnancy. If only it could have lasted a little longer. After we had snuggled for awhile in each other's arms, Daniel kissed my ear.

'I would like to love you again,' he whispered.

'But what about protection, you are not using anything.'

Donata had enlightened me about 'raincoats.'

'It's alright, just go and wash yourself, and nothing can happen.'

When I stood in the hall, wearing only my coat, I saw light under the landlady's door. I quietly opened the bathroom door, slipped in, and locked it. I went to the basin and turned on the hot water. A washcloth – there wasn't one. I took off my coat, stepped into the bathtub, and turned on the hot tap. Only cold ran out. Of course, the boiler wasn't heated. Soap – there was a tiny sliver in the dish. One of the other tenants must have felt it wasn't worth taking back to his room. The cold water made me shiver. The splinter of soap slipped through my fingers and swam down the drain. Shit ! A knock on the door made my heart race.

'Who is in there?' The voice of the landlady! I stood shivering, dripping, motionless. Better not answer . . . just keep quiet . . . the door is locked. Another hard knock . . . I stood still – frozen . . . some angry mumbling . . . then footsteps up the hall . . . knocking . . . and her voice again.

'Herr Moser, I've told you repeatedly, no girls after dark! Make sure your visitor leaves right away!'

'I'm sorry Frau Kratz, I'll take care of it.'

When it was quiet in the hall, I tiptoed back into my lover's room.

'Wait,' he whispered, 'sit down on the bed and don't move.'

He opened his door.

'Come on Annabel, you have to leave. I'll take you downstairs,' Daniel called out. He opened the apartment door, thumped down the flight of stairs, and I heard him shout, '*Auf Wiedersehen*, see you tomorrow!' In a couple of seconds he came rushing up again. He closed the apartment door with a bang, slipped into his room, and locked it.

'Now we are safe,' he smiled. He jumped into bed and pulled me under the cover.

'You're ice cold, Annabel Liebling! I'll have to warm you up all over again.' I had no objections.

We got dressed with the first light of dawn and sneaked out of the house. Daniel took me to my streetcar stop. The car was busy – people were going to work. I found a seat in a corner and waved goodbye to my love.

A letter from my father was waiting for me in my/Gerd's room. My stepmama had fallen off the ladder while taking down the dining-room curtains, and had broken a leg and injured one of her wrists. The doctor had ordered complete rest. 'I would love to have you home, Anna. Can you get away for a week?' Papa wrote. 'You know your Mama. She'll never keep still. Once I'm off to work, she'll hobble around and her leg and wrist will have no chance to heal. Let me know you'll come.' How could I refuse? I knew from experience that my stepmother couldn't tolerate hired help. Things had to be done her way. Her home was her castle.

I was torn. On one hand, I knew I had to help out my father - I wanted to. On the other, how could I leave Daniel, Daniel whom I loved, whom I adored, who had made love to me on two occasions! Leaving him now meant handing him over to Bruna, the dragoness, the bitch, the slut! I was sure she would lure him back with some of her perverted sexual practices – or her money. Her parents were wealthy, and Daniel was poor. I had nothing to offer but my heart, and I didn't even know how to do that. I threw myself on the bed and howled like an injured dog, I couldn't stop myself. I pulled the covers over my head and howled some more. Finally, the darkness and the warmth did their thing. I fell asleep.

The next morning I trudged over to the lodgings I had been fortunate to find, and paid the first month's rent. Gerd had let me know by postcard that he would be back the following week. He didn't forget to mention his former suggestion of spending a night in his bed with him. His 'personal problem' must have come to a satisfactory solution, judging by the tone of his message.

I went to the school and asked for a leave of absence due to family reasons. It was granted. I hung around hoping to run into Daniel so I could tell him I would be back in no time. Daniel my love, no need to sleep with Bruna! I'll be back – and I'll love you, love you more than anybody ever has or ever will!

He didn't show up.

I had to take my nagging doubts, my brooding anxiety home with me.

Chapter 10

I didn't care about coming home, about being with my Papa. I didn't care about the search at the border, and all the *Volkspolizisten* with their guns. East-West relations were at a low point once again, and as a result the border check was more degrading than ever. I didn't care. My grief over Daniel swallowed every other thought – my broken heart made me immune to any other emotion.

I stared out of the compartment window with blind eyes. In my mind's eye I saw Bruna, the snake, curling herself around Daniel, squeezing him tighter and tighter into her embrace. Why didn't he struggle to free himself – why didn't he scream? Don't give in Daniel, don't! I'll be back, my love, and I'll love you much more than she ever will.

Next stop Hanover, the loudspeaker announced. My darling Papa would be there, waiting for me on the platform. How to greet him? How to hide my heartache? He was used to my happy embrace, to my joy in seeing him! Pull yourself together Anna – sparkle.

I needn't have worried. His familiar face, his welcoming arms wiped away my grief. I hugged him and kissed him on both cheeks, as was my habit. Without any effort I turned into his darling little princess, the Champagne Queen, his loving daughter.

While driving through the familiar countryside to our home, Papa gave me instructions. Mama wasn't, according to doctor's orders, allowed to put any weight on her left leg, which was in a cast, or to use her right arm, which was strapped to her chest. 'I want you to report any infractions to me,' he said. '*Jawohl Herr Hauptmann*,' was my answer. We laughed. We both knew there was nothing he or I could do if she disobeyed.

I didn't mind running the household. Mama, to my surprise, was quite cooperative. In a way she seemed to enjoy her invalid status. She graciously allowed us to spoil her. Shopping, cooking, cleaning, all those boring household tasks kept me busy during the day. Daniel entered my mind frequently, but he was displaced by more substantial concerns, such as the stew boiling over and making a filthy mess over the entire stove. Nights were different. Alone in my bed my mind insisted on staying with him. Why had he wanted to be with me when he had Bruna? Why did Bruna need the attention of two men? It didn't make sense. I had one dream so vivid I couldn't shake it off all day. I was lying in bed with Daniel. He was kissing me, caressing me, about to make love to me. I was melting in his arms. Suddenly the door opened. People came streaming in, our entire drama class. They sat down on the bed, on the floor, propped themselves against the walls. I expected Daniel to shoo them away, to comfort me, but he didn't. He was swallowed up by the general commotion.

It wasn't only Daniel I couldn't put out of my mind – the scene in his bathroom kept haunting me. Had it been enough to wash myself after we made love? I counted the days on the calendar. Oh God, my period was due! But it didn't happen! – I waited, in utter agony, for three more days. Nothing. Had I miscounted? I wasn't used to keeping track - there had been no need in the past. What was I to do? Gerd's girlfriend in Düsseldorf, whom he had made pregnant, had tried hot baths and rum toddies, I remembered. It hadn't worked for her – maybe it would for me. I bought a bottle of rum, hid it in my room. All evening long I fidgeted about doing jobs that didn't need doing, like washing the kitchen floor for a second time, and I prayed for night to come. Madame Cloutot, if she saw the state I was in, would remind me to breathe from the centre, focus on my centre and my nervousness would vanish. I tried – but it made little difference. The thought of what might be happening in my centre churned my stomach into a knot.

Finally, finally, the clock struck ten. My father, who had been relaxing with a glass of beer and the daily newspaper, closed the paper and got off his chair.

'I guess I'll turn in,' he said. 'Sleep well, Anna, you seem restless.'

'I'm worried about missing out in school. An agent was supposed to come soon,' I lied. 'Maybe I'll have a hot bath, that'll calm me down.'

'If it helps you . . . I hope it won't disturb your Mama. She needs her rest.'

My hot toddy was so strong I had to add two more teaspoons of sugar to make it palatable. The bath water was so hot, my body turned as red as a lobster. I made another toddy before I went to bed. The room was racing around me when I put my head on the pillow – what a sensation! There were two identical lamps on my night table! Amazing! I closed my eyes. Now I could feel my bed rise up and float in the air. I was Aladdin on his flying carpet, only one difference – I didn't get anywhere.

'Anna, get up, I have to leave for work.' Why was my father screaming?

'Don't scream, Papa, please . . . I'm coming . . .'

'I'm not screaming. Are you alright?'

'Yes . . . yes, I'm fine . . . I'll be right there.'

My head felt like a balloon filled with water. Everything was moving inside. I heard Mama's voice. Oh no, she was up! I dragged myself into the kitchen.

'I'm sorry, but I don't feel well, I've got cramps . . .' Didn't I wish I had! I hoped to fool my father with my excuse. I was afraid he might recognize the signs of a severe hang-over.

I managed to get Mama to sit down in her wheelchair and made breakfast for the two of them. Just the smell of food made my stomach heave. Coffee, yes, coffee was good.

After my father had left, I dashed into the bathroom – nothing. Scarlett O'Hara had lost her baby when she fell down the stairs – long, wide, thickly carpeted stairs. In comparison, ours were rather short and narrow – and hard, no carpet, just old linoleum and metal trim. Still, I had to try. I stood on top ready to let myself fall. My knees buckled, my body tumbled forward – I closed my eyes. When I opened them again I found myself hanging on the rail just three steps down. The survival instinct! Damn! And yet . . . something had to be done . . . something.

Mama was dozing in her chair. Her leg, with that awkward cast, had deprived her of a good night's sleep. I slipped down into the cellar. I rummaged around till I found a rope. I tested it – too long. I looked up – was the ceiling high enough – the rope sufficiently heavy? I looped it at the ends – and jumped. Like riding a bike, your muscles don't forget how to jump rope. I easily got into a rhythm. Some of the old rhymes came back to me.

One, two, buckle your shoe,
Three, four, Bruna is a whore.

....

Twenty-five, twenty-six, don't play tricks.

....

Hundred-seven, hundred-eight, I am late, late, late.

....

Fivehundred-eleven I won't go to heaven.

....

Onethousandfiftyfour, no more, no more, no more . . .

I collapsed on the floor. My chest was heaving, my head was throbbing, my legs were screaming – Mama was calling me.

'Anna, what have you been doing? I heard noises in the cellar – was that you?'

'Just did my exercises,' I panted. 'It's part of our training... I'll just wash my face, Mama . . .' I fled into the bathroom. I was sweating so hard I felt damp all over . . . maybe? No luck, nothing.

The next day I felt soreness in my breasts. I dug out our Medical Encyclopedia, which my father still kept hidden behind a row of books. Soreness is a sure sign of pregnancy, I read with horror. What was I going to do? How could I have been so careless? It didn't matter any more if Daniel loved me, or if I ever saw him again. Not to be pregnant, that's all that mattered.

My darling Papa couldn't understand why I had tears in my eyes when I boarded the train back to Berlin. 'Don't worry about leaving us, Anna, your Mama knows now that she has to have help. I'm sure she'll get along with Frau Beyer. That woman strikes me as a person who likes to please.' He squeezed my hand. He was standing on the platform – I was leaning out the window. The tears started to dribble down my cheeks.

'Anna, is there something else? Are they not treating you well at the school? Are you lonely? Remember your dream of becoming a great star . . . remember how you won the Champagne Contest? You are an attractive girl, Anna. You can make your dream come true. Here,' he handed me a cheque, 'a little extra for your help. Buy yourself a pretty dress.'

I was glad the train started to move. I might have broken down and spilled the whole miserable story. He cared so much – but he would never understand. His daughter was a good girl. She would fall in love one day and marry. Sex, for my father, didn't exist without marriage.

My disastrous condition had made me forget that Gerd would be back and I had to move my things out of his space. I hated to face Gerd, but even more his landlady. I was afraid I might break down in tears if she mentioned Daniel.

I kept looking out the window at the fast-moving countryside. Horses, cows, old, isolated farmhouses – these sights used to delight me. Not now! A dark cloud had settled over me, a gloom no pleasant pictures could penetrate.

Chapter 11

To my relief, Gerd's landlady was out when I arrived to pick up my belongings. Gerd, charming as always, repeated his offer. He was in high spirits – I was sure he wasn't going to be a father. Should I ask him how he had solved his 'private affair'? I would have to confess that I had read his letters. Impossible! I had been voted 'most trusted student' in a survey we did in psychology class. I rejected Gerd's offer, grabbed my things and escaped into the night.

The first morning back in school I had a fencing class. I knew I wouldn't have to face Daniel. He didn't take fencing. Donata greeted me with a hug.

'You look tired, Annabel,' she said. 'Did your father make you work hard?'

Tears rushed into my eyes before I could answer. Donata squeezed my arm.

'Tell me after class,' she whispered.

'Fräulein Lambert, I know you have missed some classes, but now that you are present, please pay attention.' The fencing instructor glared at me. Everybody looked at me. I looked for a hole to creep in and vanish. I forced myself to go on with the exercises: en garde – lunge – thrust! My rapier escaped my grip and with an ugly, harsh clatter rolled along the floor. Once again I had the class's full attention – all eyes on me! I could hear my classmates' thoughts: 'Pregnant . . . pregnant . . . little Miss Proper has a bun in the oven.' Did it show? I pulled in my stomach. 'Poor Annabel,' I heard them think, 'she seemed to be such a decent girl, so well behaved . . . look at her now . . . she's no better than a whore.'

Donata pulled me into the garden as soon as the class was over. We crouched down under a weeping willow, and I spilled my misery.

'Oh Annabel, what are you going to do? Daniel has left the school, do you know? He's gone home. I think he has given up on acting. Who knows what he is doing now? You can't have his baby.'

'I don't want his baby . . . I don't want any baby . . . I can't be pregnant . . . I can't!' I shouted.

'I don't know of anybody who could help you, Annabel . . . except . . . Madame Cloutot! I heard the old geezer call her a sorceress, because of her outlandish methods, I guess, and the way she dresses! That turban, and all those scarves that flutter around her like bats. You know she likes you. Maybe she has an idea of what you can do.'

My hands were shaking when I rang madame's bell. She welcomed me with a smile, and asked me in. When she opened the door wide I took a step back. I was blinded by the light! Her apartment was white, all white. Walls, carpet, all the furniture, even the cushions on the sofa, all white. It looked fantastic, unreal! I expected the Snow Queen to appear and wave her icicle wand over me.

'Have you seen my star student, Maria W. at the Schiller Theater?' Madame Cloutot wasn't one for small talk. 'You absolutely have to see her. She acted from her centre! Her body was resting in her pelvis, and every movement, every emotion erupted from there. She made me proud. She showed the world that my method is right and unsurpassable. Annabel, look at your posture,' she dragged me to a full-length mirror. 'How are you standing . . . tilt your pelvis . . . open your chest . . . grow, grow . . . think upward . . . breathe . . . breathe . . .'

I straightened up and took a deep breath.

'No, Annabel, you are not in your centre – lie down.'

I obeyed. Madame knelt down beside me.

'Drop your lumbar spine,' she slid her hand under the small of my back. 'Pull your thighs together . . . pull them into your centre . . . relax your stomach . . . more . . . you are not letting go Annabel! What is it? Why are you crying?'

'I'm pregnant . . . I know I am . . . I don't know what to do . . .'

Madame jumped up. 'Come sit with me,' she pulled me over to a chaise-longue. 'Breathe out,' she put her hand on my stomach, 'out . . . out,' she gently pushed her hand into my tummy. 'Let all the worry go. Breathe it away . . . away . . .' she sing-songed. After awhile she stood up and faced me.

'Why are you sure, Annabel? Have you seen a doctor?'

'No, not yet . . .' I mumbled, 'but I should have had my period a week ago, and my breasts are sore . . . and I'm never late,' which was an assumption.

'Too early to worry,' Madame stated with authority. 'Do your exercises, abdominal breathing, twenty rounds at a time, relax and envision your body doing the regular thing. I'm sure it's stress that prevents the uterus from letting go.'

She turned and went to her kitchen. I heard her opening and closing some cupboards. She returned with a tiny cloth pouch.

'Make a tea from the herbs in this pouch,' she advised. 'Drink it before you go to bed. You'll be fine Annabel. No more worrying . . . promise.' I did. But as much as I wanted to believe her, I had doubts about her potion. It had a faint mint smell to it.

That night, in my new landlady's kitchen, I prepared Madame Cloutot's tea. The subtle mint smell was misleading, the mixture tasted horrible. Never mind, all secret potions tasted bitter, I knew it from fairy tales. They weren't concocted for your taste buds but for miracles to happen. I drank three cups, gulping them down one after the other.

'Oh, you like Valerian root tea, Fräulein Lambert,' my landlady sniffed like a dog as she entered the kitchen. 'Do you have a drop left for me? It makes me sleep well.' She took a cup from her cupboard and poured the last little bit of liquid out of the teapot. 'Yes,' she smiled, 'undoubtedly Valerian with just a hint of mint. Tastes bitter but makes you sleep like a baby. Good night, Fräulein Lambert. We'll both sleep tight I'm sure.'

So that's what Madame's secret potion was – Valerian root with a hint of mint! She *was* a sorceress. She knew about the placebo effect. I had to smile. I couldn't wait to tell Donata. For the first time in a week I did sleep soundly. I woke up relaxed, and before the dark pregnancy cloud could catch me, I got down on the floor and did the exercises. I concentrated so hard on the movement of my breath and the vision of my body doing the regular thing, I got so relaxed, I forgot my desperate state for minutes at a time.

For two days I practiced. I did so many rounds of abdominal breathing my tummy felt sore. My visualizations were so hypnotic, I dozed off a few times. And on the third day, when I was about to give up hope, my period appeared.

Life, once again, was full of promise.

Chapter 12

Now that our graduation was only days away, the boys were conducting another unofficial survey. Question: How many of your female co-students have you slept with? I wondered if Jürgen's attempt counted as a conquest – by rights, it should. He had got me into his bed. That there hadn't been any action was entirely my fault.

I was glad Daniel had left and I didn't have to face my handsome, troublesome lover. He had been careful after all – it would have been easy to fall in love with him all over again. But he was gone. He had become as unobtainable as Laurence Olivier. Never mind the short time we had spent together - never mind that I hadn't really got to know him. He had taken residence in a small corner of my heart and would live there, young and handsome, forever.

I was taken aback when one night my hostess announced a visitor. I had just returned from school and was about to feel sorry for myself for being alone and unloved. A visitor? Who could it be? Only Donata knew my new address. I was stunned to see Gerd come swaggering down the hall towards me. We hadn't talked at all after I had fled his room, but I had learned from his adored ethereal beauty that he had used the time away to audition at a prestigious theatre in Düsseldorf. The company had offered him a two-year contract. The news of his employment had spread with hurricane speed through the school. The boys envied him – the girls praised him. His success didn't surprise me – he wasn't only handsome and charming, but talented and ambitious.

'Annabel, sorry to disturb you,' he invited himself into my room and closed the door. 'Can you help me out? Will you lend me your copy of Goethe's *Faust* please? I'm cast as Valentin in the Düsseldorf production. I seem to have misplaced my copy – or did you take it away with your things by accident?'

It turned out that he wasn't looking for a copy of *Faust.* He wanted to put another feather on his cap.

'I think you are a very attractive girl, Annabel, but you appear to hold back on stage – as I have told you many a time. You need to forget about your upbringing and your beliefs and become the character in the play.' Gerd sat down on the bed beside me. 'You need to let go, surrender to your role, to make it real. I can help you, trust me.' He drew me close and kissed me.

'I know you like me,' he whispered, 'I'm all yours if you want me.'

Dream on Gerd, dream on! I'm not going to give you the satisfaction of another conquest! He worked up a lot of steam and was ready to go, but I kept my underwear firmly in place – which wasn't an easy task. I had to draw on my entire cache of willpower to halt the natural flow of things.

A knock on the door solved my dilemma.

'I have a piece of freshly baked *Apfelstrudel* in the kitchen for you, Fräulein Lambert,' my landlady announced. I knew she was concerned about my morals. She didn't like me to spoil my, in her eyes, spotless record. I appreciated her fussing this time. It made it easier to tell Gerd he had to leave.

'You are more interested in apple strudel than in making love to me?'

'It looks like it,' I grinned.

Alone again in my little room, I should have felt as triumphant as Napoleon after the battle of Austerlitz. I'm sorry to say, I didn't. What had I won? Another lonely night! Why was love so complicated? How did you make a man love you after sex? Why did sex mean so much to men? I liked kissing and cuddling – and you couldn't get pregnant from that. I promised myself to keep my desire in check. I wouldn't lie down again for a man as willingly as I had for Daniel. It was too . . . disturbing.

I would have preferred to arrive in my sleepy hometown in the middle of the night, so nobody would see me. My return reminded me of the story of a cat, who sets out for a feast in the barn and returns, exhausted, with an empty stomach. What had I learned in these two years of training, what had I achieved? I had at long last lost my virginity and I had learned about men. I had been lonely, sad, anxious and – happy, for a few hours. I had learned a bit of fencing, and some historic dances. I had learned about Sigmund Freud and his belief that most habits and obsessions had a grounding in early sexuality. Maybe my poor sex life was the reason for my 'average' performances on stage. Maybe Gerd was right, I needed sexual experience. Sadly, there wasn't anybody around I could fall in love with. Never mind love, I had to get out and find a job, I had to prove to myself, and to my Papa, that my dreams were not the fantastic imaginations of a girl who had been brought up on fairy tales, had read too many sentimental novels, and watched too many romantic films! I had to get a job.

Nobody had told me how degrading and depressing auditions were. In the school, people at least knew my name, now at the auditions I became Fräulein what's-your-name, an anonymous, generic entity, one in a million, hurry up, don't waste my time kind of person. I travelled by train, slept in more or less comfortable Bed & Breakfast places, where the owners were more or less friendly, the breakfast more or less substantial, and where I felt homesick and abandoned every night. I presented myself on empty stages, in front of a black vastness that sometimes revealed the outline of a human face. Out of the depth of that darkness a human voice would urge me to start or stop. 'We have other candidates to see. You'll hear from us if we want you,' was the standard answer. Nobody cared that I had just acted my heart out. The directors didn't have to be friendly or compassionate. They had an endless supply to choose from. For the first time I questioned my ambition. Was I cut out for this profession? I remembered Oma telling me to flirt with my teachers to gain their attention – but how do you flirt with a man you don't get to see? The answer was appearance, my appearance on stage.

I could make myself look so . . . so provocative they wouldn't be able to ignore me. I still had the blouse I had bought at *Wertheim*'s for the dance at the Arts Club. It had worked for Robert. It had made him abandon his fashion model girlfriend for me! I dug out the blouse, and cut the neckline a few centimeters lower. I shortened the hem on my skirt to just above the knee. I bought a pair of black stockings at the only clothing store in our town. I was lucky – they were leftovers from the last Carneval season.

A highly rated theatre in Hamburg had answered my application and asked me for an audition. I arrived the day prior to the date and checked into a B&B. I didn't sleep well. Would my plan work? Would I be able to pull it off? I was up early – lots of time to get made up. Green eye shadow like Elke, who had lured Mephistopheles into her bed. Black lines around the eyes, Bruna the snake's specialty. Three coats of mascara, and a bright red lipstick like the women in the new American Technicolour movies were wearing. My high-heeled shoes hurt my toes – no matter. I walked up and down in my room practicing a swaggering gait. I tripped twice and nearly cracked my ankle, no matter – somebody down in that black hole would notice me today! To match my outfit, I had learned the part Bruna had studied at the school – Sabrina in Thornton Wilder's *The Skin of our Teeth*. She was what men called a 'dish'. Breakfast over, the owner of my B&B took me aside.

'You strike me as a well brought-up girl, Fräulein Lambert – for an actress. Only remember, you are in a harbour city, which has a famous red light district, the Reeperbahn. You might have heard of it? The way you look today, some sailors might get the wrong idea. I suggest you wear your coat over your outfit and just keep on walking if a sailor approaches you.' Her remarks reassured me. I would be noticed today!

I was ready. When the voice out of the black vastness urged me to begin, I flipped my imaginary feather duster wildly through space, pretending to dust the imaginary furniture. Then I stopped by the imaginary window, leaned forward by sticking out my bum, gave it a little wriggle and said,

> OH, OH, OH! Six o'clock and the master not home yet. Pray God nothing serious has happened to him crossing the Hudson River. If anything happened to him . . .

I swaggered away from the window and, swinging my hips as I walked around the imaginary furniture pretending to dust, delivered my text in a high-pitched voice. I had just said,

> The fact is I don't know what will become of us . . .

when out of the darkness came a snickering sound, then a couple of chuckles, followed by a forceful STOP. I heard whispering, then footsteps, and in a couple of seconds a man materialized on stage.

'Thank you, Fräulein . . . that was quite entertaining. A word of advice: Sabrina is not your genre. Behind all the make-up and the exaggerated posturing you are, I believe, an animated but innocent girl.'

He stifled a chuckle. 'Not a Sabrina – definitely not!' He disappeared into thin air as quickly as the magician's rabbit.

I took my hostess' advice. I buttoned up my coat and strolled back to my lodgings to pick up my suitcase. A couple of catcalls from some workman on a scaffold were all the attention I got.

I hid the blouse, skirt and black stockings in the bottom of my case, donned the neat dress I had bought myself from the money my Papa had given me, and boarded the train to Aachen where another audition was looming. The city, close to the Dutch border, had been the first to be bombed and the first to be conquered by Allied Forces. I also knew Aachen from history class. Charlemagne had been crowned Holy Roman Emperor there, and the Aachener Dome was regarded as one of the most beautiful cathedrals in Europe. What I didn't know was that through all the centuries, the city hadn't lost its status as a bastion of Catholicism.

A new theatre was under construction, I learned, so my audition took place in temporary quarters – in a bright room on a small rehearsal stage. I was flabbergasted when the artistic director introduced himself and asked me personal questions. How old ? Married? Engaged? Did I live with my parents? He was polite and friendly. He also had a different approach to auditions.

'Fräulein Lambert, I want you to imagine you are in a room and fire breaks out in the building. You see smoke curling in under the door; you hear the crackling of burning wood. You rush to the door – it is locked. You are trapped. What do you do?'

I pictured the flames licking at the door, I smelled the acrid, foul smoke, and I went berserk! I pounded against the door, I attempted to climb up the walls to an imagined window, I screamed for help, I raged, I cried for my father. At the end I collapsed on the floor and whimpered. I was exhausted. I was sure I had given a hell of a performance.

'You forgot one thing, Fräulein Lambert, one very important thing,' the director's calm voice made me lift my head. 'What is it?'

'Hm . . . I should have covered my nose so I wouldn't inhale the smoke?' I ventured.

'No, that's not what I am looking for. Who could have helped you – who is always there to help us?'

I racked my brain . . . and then it struck me . . .

'God,' I cried, ' you mean I should have asked for God's help?'

'Yes, Fräulein Lambert, you should have prayed, prayed on your knees! Do you not believe in God?'

'I do, oh ja, I do,' I answered eagerly.

'Then get down on your knees and pray!' he ordered.

'God, holy Lord, God in heaven, help me . . .'

'Halt,' he shouted, 'stop. Whom do we ask for help, who is our intercessor?'

I was dumbfounded. What was he after? Oh please God, tell me!

'Christ, Jesus Christ our Saviour! He will intercede for us. Have you not been baptized?' He looked at me like I was an alien about to infiltrate his holy city.

'I was christened, my father told me – and I went to confirmation classes . . . '

'Ah', he screamed, 'you are a Protestant – no wonder you don't know a proper prayer! Did you see our cathedral? It was built by true believers, only true believers can produce a work of such gigantic beauty. Goodbye Fräulein Lambert, my secretary will let you know.' He turned on the spot and walked out the door. I stood on the stage alone, aghast. Then I brushed off my dress, tidied up my hair, collected my coat and handbag and walked right out of the place. There was one good aspect to this abominable meeting. No need to wait for yet another phone call – there wouldn't be one. Guaranteed.

Chapter 13

1956 – 1958

I was getting desperate. June had come around, and I still had no contract, no job. All the repertory companies, highly subsidized by the government, hired actors for a full season: September to May or June. Contracts, as a rule, were signed for one or two seasons. If actors weren't hired before the summer break, there was little chance to get in – unless some person in some company got pregnant, sick, or died. My desire to stand on a big stage or in front of a camera was beginning to feel pathetic and unobtainable. I avoided leaving the house – I hated to lie to our neighbours and my former classmates about my career. I had no answer to their questions: What theatre company had hired me? Would I have to move to Hamburg or to Munich – or back to Berlin to make a movie at Tempelhof studios? What to tell them? I didn't know where I would end up! Maybe I would never become a princess in a beautiful castle! Maybe I would have to stay in the kitchen and sleep by the cinders forever?

My darling Papa sensed my doubts and voiced his own.

'There is no shame in letting this whole acting thing go, Anna. The more I hear and read about the profession, particularly the movie stars, the way they change partners . . . like ordinary people change their cars! That can't make for a happy life, I'm sure.'

My Papa was right about the film stars and their musical chairs love lives. Rita Hayworth and Agha Khan, the glamour couple who had filled the gossip columns of every newspaper, were divorced. The marriage of my adored Laurence Olivier and his beautiful wife was also falling apart. He had already found a new partner, and Vivien Leigh was having an affair with Peter Finch, another extremely attractive actor. I was sure these couples weren't heartbroken about the breakups. For actors there was no shortage of attractive, desirable partners. They didn't have to stay married to someone they no longer loved. Love – where did that get you anyway? Romeo and Juliet, Anne Boleyn and Henry VIII, that pig, Anna Karenina and her hussar, Heathcliff and Catherine, who drove him to insanity – great love affairs that had brought on nothing but death and disaster. My Papa didn't have to worry – no more stupid falling in love for me! Now that I knew all about men and sex, I would lock any desire way down into the dungeon of my brain and concentrate on my roles and my career. I had wasted enough time in Berlin on men – no more of that! Now my career would be my lover. A new surge of confidence washed over me like a warm ocean wave. I would succeed – I would rise out of the ocean like Venus – new, beautiful, and unresponsive to the lures of the flesh!

Was it my new determination or coincidence? The good fairy didn't let me rot in the kitchen after all. She waved her magic wand and presented me with a contract. Not in a beautiful castle, meaning one of the big city theatres, but in a small town close to the Dutch border. The citizens of the historic town of Cleves, famous for Anne of Cleves, fourth wife of Henry VIII, who had managed to walk away from that pig with her head firmly attached to her shoulders, were dedicated theatre enthusiasts – only there weren't enough of them to fill the theatre every night. So we invaded the villages and towns within a thirty kilometre range from our headquarters, to spread culture among the hard-working peasants and townspeople. Wherever there was a hall of some kind, we set up shop, once a month, and brought joy or confusion to the culturally and educationally deprived population. First, our truck with the sets and the costumes would arrive. The stagehands, fellows blessed with great skills and a lot of 'make do' set up the scenery. – How do you screw walls into a concrete floor? How do you build up the scenery on a twenty-by-fifteen space when it was intended for a stage measuring thirty-by-twenty-five feet? Where do you find dressing rooms for the actors when there aren't any? They managed. By the time the cast arrived, the stage was set. The stage manager, a man of endless patience and an immeasurable sense of duty, who at times had to pitch in when our male cast ran short, would give a few instructions in hushed tones: 'Make sure you don't come in contact with the walls. They'll come tumbling down like the walls of Jericho.' Or, 'Don't forget to cut your steps in half, Annabel and Marianne, when you rush up to the front of the stage in act two. Otherwise you'll end up on the lap of a first row spectator.' And often, 'Scream if you want to be heard – the acoustics are lousy.'

Our comedy performances were received with thigh slapping laughter and catcalls, while plays by Dürrenmatt, Ionesco, Pinter left the audience dumbfounded. The applause would die down before it had started. The people in the audience looked at each other and rushed across the road to the pub wondering why they had spent three marks of their hard-earned money for 'this modern nonsense.' They felt cheated. Luckily, our director had an inborn sense of fairness. The farm audience knew if they managed to sit through one of the 'educational' plays they would be rewarded with a side-splitting farce, a sentimental love story, or one of the classics by Schiller or Goethe. Nobody dared to poopooh the latter.

Our company was twelve bodies strong. Only four women, lucky me, and eight men, including the directors. Three new male actors had joined the cast with me – one a middle-aged tall thin man with a pockmarked face, the other a young man not quite as tall and heavier built, with an unremarkable face. He had straight blond hair that kept falling over his forehead and into his blue eyes. I couldn't make up my mind if one could call him handsome when he smiled. No, maybe not. Nobody handsome around! Oh, I forgot – a Freudian slip of memory – the young hero player, Remus. Heaven knows in what book he had found that name! I hated him. His looks were faultless, his personality ghastly. He dominated every conversation, criticized everyone but himself, and was a lousy actor. In no time he shacked up with the young character actress. He wooed the directors by flattering them and reporting gossip from among the cast. He reminded me of Elke at the school – I was sure he would do anything for a part he wanted.

The managing director, a rotund, jolly man of around fifty, and the head director, old and with a weathered face, treated me like a daughter. It was the third man in the triumvirate, early to mid-forties, rather short, with a boxer's broken nose, dark hair cut page-boy style, and sharp grey eyes who gave me the jitters. In his presence I shared the fear of a field mouse when the shadow of a hawk falls on it.

'They hired you without my input, Fräulein Lambert – only hope the two old men didn't make a mistake.' He looked me over as if I was a horse to be auctioned off. I was surprised he didn't ask me to open my mouth so he could inspect my teeth.

'I guess you'll do,' he finally muttered. 'Just don't behave like a star because you studied at a reputable school in Berlin. Here, you are a greenhorn, a bloody beginner – remember that.'

Josefa, the only older woman in the ensemble, married to a local photographer, took me aside. 'Don't mind him. He likes to scare new members. It's one of his tactics to keep them in line. After a few glasses of beer he's quite harmless.' She grinned like a Cheshire cat. 'He can even be charming with young female newcomers.'

Oh, why, why did I have to have so much time on my hands at the start of the season! Only rehearsals in the morning, and all night alone in my room. A cozy room, about three kilometres out of town, in a brand new house surrounded by trees, fields and clusters of forest. I liked that. The proprietress, married for only a few months, seemed delighted about her acquired state, and didn't exercise any of the protective motherliness of my Berlin landlady. I liked that too.

My room, designed as the dining-room of the house, had a floor to ceiling ceramic stove and French doors leading into the living room which, I finally figured out, had been converted into the young couple's bedroom. A heavy curtain covered my side of the French doors, and a big armoire closed them off on their side. Not a soundproof arrangement! I couldn't help hearing subdued bursts of laughter, squeals and giggles at night and sometimes in the afternoon. No wonder it took me so long to figure out what went on beyond the curtain. None of my limited sexual encounters had tickled my funny bone.

I threw myself into the practice of my art. 'Mimimimi, mamamama, momomomo . . . until my head felt like the inside of a drum. I flopped down onto the uncarpeted floor, dropped my lumbar spine, pulled my thighs together and assembled all my energy in my centre. I stood up and became a tree stretching toward the sun in perfect posture. Madame Cloutot would have been proud of me. I forced my fat tongue to fold in the middle, which I had never managed in voice class, and the tip of my tongue to touch the back of my throat. I searched for a rapier, found a metal rod in the yard, and practiced in front of the mirror: en garde – lunge – thrust - CRASH ! A thousand pieces of mirror scattered all over the floor. I knew what that meant – seven years of bad luck! Did it start immediately or was there a grace period? Did you get time off for good behaviour? I knocked on my landlady's door and right away started my apologies - voluminous apologies. At the end, my first salary, hardly enough to pay for room and food, was reduced by fifteen marks. I'm sure it was a fair price. She had seen the embarrassment and fear in my eyes and had been merciful. It took me an hour to collect all the glass fragments. I was Cinderella, back in the kitchen, picking the peas out of the ashes. No more walking barefoot, I told myself. There might be a sliver of bad luck lurking under the table or the chairs and if it pierced my flesh, I was condemned to bad luck till the end of my days.

Chapter 14

It took just three weeks of rehearsals until the two young women were coupled up – the heroine had succumbed to the invisible charms of the pockmarked face and the character actress, driven by a masochistic streak, had shacked up with the arrogant, self possessed, scheming Remus. The women had shared two seasons before my arrival and were tight friends. Now the two couples were a unit. They joked with each other in the dressing room, shared sandwiches and thermos bottles at lunchtime, and drank together at the pub at night. I was alone, left out, and reminded of Berlin. I missed Donata, I missed my Papa, I even missed my brother and my stepmother.

Werner Helwig, the blond young man, wasn't as left out as I. He could joke around with the rest of the male cast. But – he also started to pay attention to me. We both had small parts in our opening play and so spent hours together in the dressing room waiting to be called on stage. He was a good listener, polite, and like me, came from a small town. He took to walking me home after rehearsal, though his place was just minutes from the theatre. He told me about his previous love relationship. He had broken off with a co-student at his drama school in Frankfurt. She had been 'experienced' he admitted, and had taught him the right moves. No fumbling, no embarrassment! I kept mum about my love life. I hadn't really had one.

One night when I couldn't face my loneliness, I agreed to join him at the *Burgschenke*, Cleves' popular hang-out for pretend-to-be and real artists. The entire gang was there, including the Hawk, our No.2 director. Remus had planted himself beside the Hawk. He was talking to him, whispering at times, and grinning. The Hawk, I noticed, wasn't into the conversation. He kept shooting glances at *me*. He threw the odd remark across the table.

'Your proper ways won't do here, Fräulein Lambert - loosen up, have a shot of *Genever* with your beer!' And louder, so everybody could hear it, 'I hope we haven't hired a virgin – our Young Innocent isn't sexually innocent. You are to be innocent in spirit, Fräulein Lambert, not in body – your next role requires experience.' Everybody laughed. Werner squeezed my hand under the table. I kept my mouth shut. It worked. The Hawk gave up stalking me.

Our season opener had passed without a hitch. Werner and I became friends. I was an impassioned talker, he a patient, avid listener. I knew I could confide in him. Anything I said about our colleagues - and oh, did they provide some mouth-watering gossip - would be our secret. I liked it when he walked me home at night. He had to tramp all the way back again to his room in town. True devotion. We had kissed a few times, and on one of these occasions I had told him I wasn't ready for more. Was I afraid to get sexually involved because I didn't love him? Did I not love him because he wasn't handsome, not rich, not influential, not a prince on a white horse? Still, I felt flattered – two men wanted me! The Hawk's attentions, so obviously based on the desires of the flesh - my flesh to be precise - gave me a bit of a thrill, I hated to admit. Being thus coveted made me feel snug and secure – until a cuckoo landed in my cozy nest and viciously ruffled my feathers.

After one long rehearsal I was tired, hungry, and looking forward to a meal and a snooze. I packed up my things and handed Werner my bag. He had adopted the pleasant habit of carrying it for me.

'Sorry, Annabel, I can't go with you today. Hannelore arrived last night. She's expecting me.' He kept me holding the bag, literally.

'Your girl friend? You said you had broken off with her . . . what is she doing here?'

'I'm not sure myself. She said she had to see me. She's waiting in my room right now.'

'Where did she sleep last night - with you? In your bed?' Werner tried to say something. 'Don't lie to me please, I'm sure you didn't make her sleep on the floor! And anyway you have only one pillow and one comforter. I'm sure you didn't ask your landlady for extra bedding in the middle of the night!'

'It was late, I didn't know what to do. She has no money. I couldn't throw her out on the street.'

'You better not bother with me anymore,' I hissed. 'I'll not share you! I thought we understood each other, but I was mistaken. You are no better than all the other men – you double-crossing liar!' I was hurt, I was furious! I was reminded of Daniel and Bruna, the dragoness. I wanted to hurt Werner – hurt him for all I had endured in Berlin.

When I met him that night at the bus, I ignored him. I got on, and when I spotted an empty place beside the Hawk, I plunked myself down and started a conversation. I didn't have to say much. The Hawk was full of theatre anecdotes and hilarious stories. He made me laugh out loud. I got to feel more at ease with him, and the way he played along nearly made me like him.

I kept tossing and turning on my mattress that night making more squeaking noises than my two turtledoves next door. The whole blasted dilemma struck me as déjà-vu. Robbed of my lover by another experienced snake, another dragoness, another man-eater! My lover – a lie. I had kept him at bay because I wasn't sure I wanted him. I was sure now: I wanted him, he was mine, I couldn't bear losing him!

Hannelore stayed for two nights. She accompanied Werner to the bus the next day. I tried not to look at her, just glanced with one eye – she was pretty, darn. Werner came towards me – did he want to introduce her? I turned and jumped onto the bus. The Hawk had reserved a seat for me next to him. Good, I would show Werner – I was ready to show him! What - I wasn't quite sure. I laughed and giggled and flirted with the Hawk. I overacted like an amateur. When he put his hand on my knee while I was roaring with laughter, I sobered up. I got scared he might get the wrong idea.

'You like him, don't you?' he said suddenly. I looked at him blank-faced. 'Werner - you love him, right?' I was glad it was dark in the bus. He might have seen the blood rising to my cheeks. I couldn't think of anything to say – I wasn't that sure. 'A pity,' he said, 'I'm not used to being rejected by young newcomers.'

It happened to be a dark night, but my thoughts were darker as I found myself walking alone to my wobbly nest. Shit, shit, shit, shit . . . I swore. It was the first thing I had learned at the theatre – swearing. Everybody did it, and shit was the most popular word in an actor's vocabulary. It was a good word, when you were really mad. It helped to get rid of your anger - about a play, about another actor, about our meager wages, about the unappreciative peasants, about Konrad Adenauer and his government, etc., etc. Shit, shit, shit! I screamed into the dark. And once more s-h-i-i-i-i-t !!! Miraculously, my murderous thoughts vanished. The tears, which had been ready to flood my face, dried up. SHIT – what a wonderful, healing word.

No rehearsal for me the next morning! More time to feel abandoned, forgotten, betrayed. I wrote a long letter to my Papa, a letter full of lies and pretensions. It was enough that I felt miserable; he deserved to feel proud of me – as I had promised he would. I wrote a letter to my brother. I hadn't heard from Hans in weeks. I was sure Christa, his dragon wife, didn't give him a chance to visit with me. I was just about to seal the letters, when the doorbell rang. I heard my landlady clomping along the hall, she must have been wearing her wooden clogs again, heard her opening the front door, then steps clomping back down the hall, and a knock on my door. My heart jumped into my throat – could it be Werner? I opened the door.

'Someone to see you, Fräulein Lambert . . . doesn't want to come in.' Can't be Werner! He would have come in! Maybe not – he'd never been inside the house.

It was Werner!

'Just came to tell you Hannelore left this afternoon,' he started. 'She won't be back. We had a long talk . . . she knows we are finished. I'm sorry if her visit upset you.' He looked me straight in the eye, and I saw so much genuine fear in his, so much childlike unhappiness, I couldn't be mad at him. I remembered the anxiety and the despair I had sunk into when I had been unsure of Daniel's love. I didn't have the heart to let him suffer.

'Thanks for telling me,' I said in the most quiet, controlled voice I could muster. No need to go overboard – and show my joy.

'I'll see you at the bus tonight then.' He turned and with one leap jumped over the garden gate. I allowed myself a deep sigh. I closed the door and danced back into my room. I waltzed around my table, humming *Tales from the Vienna Woods*, bumped myself twice on a chair, and collapsed finally on my bed breathing hard and smiling like an idiot at the ceiling.

Chapter 15

We made love every afternoon in my bed. Having a man stay overnight wasn't appreciated by any landlady, and in as small a town as Cleves, it was better to respect the rules. Love after the mid-day meal was a special treat – more delicious, more satisfying than the sweetest dessert. And there was sufficient time to complete our sensuous pleasure with a regenerating nap. We arrived for the night's performance content and refreshed.

At our first encounter, after extensive foreplay, I had been ready, but Werner wasn't. There was no poking, because he had nothing to poke me with. A replay of my night with Jürgen in Berlin – roles reversed? Was this going to be another catastrophic encounter? Had my seven years of bad luck begun? Werner apologized, but wasn't too concerned. He didn't know my history!

'I'm so overwhelmed – I have waited for this for so long – give me a little time,' he said. Luckily, there was no performance that night. We lay naked in each other's arms, under the soft, warm eiderdown. We talked, we kissed, he stroked me expertly, and then he was ready. I closed my eyes and let him proceed. Before I could even whisper my concern about pregnancy, he told me he knew how to take care. And he did. Thank you Hannelore! His lack of an erection at the start was the sign of a sensitive man, a man with deep feelings, I told myself. He wasn't just after another conquest – he cared for me.

Soon, I cooked our mid-day meal in my room. We bought a hot plate, a pan and a pot. Our prop man gave us a couple of plates, slightly chipped, and some cutlery, slightly bent. We spent all our waking hours together. No seven years of bad luck! I felt like the luckiest person on the planet. I had a boyfriend who was mine, only mine. I knew I could trust him – the two of us against the world – I had read that somewhere – now I felt it. For the first time I could open my heart to my lover – I could talk to him as much as I wanted, and about what I wanted. I could share every thought that came into my head. I could touch him whenever I felt like it, wherever I wanted. How long had I waited for this kind of closeness? Now it was mine – mine!

My cup ran over when I got the lead in a sophisticated comedy – and I got scared. It was a dream part – a part young actresses killed for. Did I deserve such good fortune? Werner said I did. He said I was ideal for the role. Sure, nobody else in our company was suitable. There were just a couple of drawbacks. The two men cast as my lovers were of the homosexual orientation, though not with each other, and the Hawk was directing. I shooed away any dark thoughts. After the laughs I had shared with him on the bus, he was my friend. I had nothing to fear.

Rehearsals were going well. My partners knew how to act and I learned fast. I had to overcome the strange feeling that neither had the slightest interest in me offstage – never mind how seductively I wrapped myself around them in the play. One of the men was an established comic actor. I learned how to get a laugh from him. The third man involved, the Hawk, was no longer laughing. Now that Werner and I were lovers, his jealousy turned green. He sniped at me for no reason. I was determined not to react. The dialogue was brilliant, the play so well constructed, I wallowed in the glory of it all. I didn't allow him to poison my joy.

What to wear?

Our jolly manager was ready for my question. 'In a contemporary play you are obliged to provide your own wardrobe, Fräulein Lambert,' he told me.

'Ingeborg is the wife of a wealthy man – I don't have the kind of clothes she would wear.'

'Can you sew?'

'A little . . .'

'I'll get you a sewing machine, Annabel, as a special favour, just for you. Let it be our secret,' he touched his nose.

At our full dress rehearsal, one of my dresses wasn't quite finished. It was held in place by pins.

'Don't hug me too tightly,' I whispered to one of my lovers. Fat chance for him to be carried away!

The rehearsal was over. The Hawk swung himself onto the stage with an exaggerated youthfulness, which made him drop his notepad. He didn't bother to pick it up, but left that task to the prop man. He told my two lovers a couple of minor alterations ending with 'You were marvelous, superb – keep it that way tonight.' I fiddled with the pins in my dress and pricked a finger. 'Ouch!' The Hawk paid no attention. He ignored me. He gave lengthy instructions to the lighting crew and the soundman. I waited with a pounding heart. He started to walk away, then turned.

'Fräulein Lambert, your performance was acceptable,' he muttered, 'except in the second act when you were showing off your new dress to your lover. You were twirling around exposing your underwear to the audience. This sort of cheap appeal is not accepted here. Make sure your private parts are well covered tonight.' End of comment.

Everybody looked at me – what will she do? I did nothing – but in my mind I gave him a good kick in the groin!

When the curtain rose and I, in my home-sewn pantsuit, slipped into my role, all private thoughts were forgotten. I was carefree, playful Ingeborg, who juggled her two adoring men with skill and charm. And the audience went with me all the way. They giggled and laughed and sighed – and applauded with enthusiasm when the curtain came down. I felt like the whole world belonged to me. I loved everyone, particularly my darling Papa who had come a long way to see me perform. He squeezed me tightly in front of the entire cast, after the performance. Oh, how I loved him! How happy it made me to see the pride in his eyes. I wanted him to stay, to celebrate with us, but he couldn't. My stepmama wasn't feeling well – he had to get back home as soon as possible.

As usual there was a party at the *Burgschenke.* The place was packed. Regular citizens of Cleves filled the tables. Glasses of beer and *Genever* appeared in front of us – gestures of appreciation. The audience felt the need to thank us for the pleasure we had provided. I was overwhelmed with gratitude. I was flying through a cloudless sky. The Hawk, never one to gauge his drinking, became soft and sentimental and confessed his love for me. I had imbibed sufficiently myself to not take offence – to the contrary. My teenage dream of running a salon where important men would come to adore me flashed through my intoxicated mind. Nothing was impossible – not in the state I was in.

Midnight had long passed when Werner and I started out for the long walk to my place. I deeply inhaled the fresh air, which scrambled my brain and made my bones feel like rubber. A wonderful feeling! I took Werner's arm to steady myself.

'I hope the Hawk didn't get the wrong impression,' he muttered.

'Why, my darling sweetheart, why would you say that?'

'Because you were flirting with him . . .'

'So what! He knows I love only you . . . only youuuuu . . .' I sang. I tried to stay close to the curb – an impossible task. A most mysterious power made me drift into the middle of the road again and again.

'You are drunk! How many *Genevers* did you pour down your throat?' Werner tried to rescue me from possible traffic on the road.

'Which one of you is t-al-king,' I stuttered. 'There are t-t-wo of you . . . or three?'

'Come take my arm again, I'll guide you,' Werner tried to hold onto me.

'Away . . . away, double-headed creature! Don't interfere with the Queen of Merriment.' I sat down on the curb and howled with laughter.

Werner, in an attempt to lift me up, wobbled and fell on top of me.

'You are drunk,' I shouted triumphantly, 'drunk . . . drunk . . . drunk!'

After several attempts he managed to achieve an upright position, and tried to help me into one.

'Away . . . away . . . remove yourself . . . ACTOR! I can only be lifted by a PRINCE, a prince on a white horse, prefer-r-r-ebly.'

'No prince with or without a horse would have you in this state, madam,' Werner bowed low, grabbed my arm and pulled me up. For a split second we were in danger of toppling over and landing in a pile of horse shit. But no, my knight stayed firmly planted in the upright position. He dragged, pulled and pushed me, step by step, to my house. After some rummaging I found the key in my purse, but it wouldn't fit in the lock.

'Who switched my key?' I shouted.

'Hush . . . you don't want to deprive our giggling bride of her night's rest. Let me try.'

After some swearing, some fumbling, and Werner's admirable patience, the key turned in the lock. I staggered into the hall pulling Werner in with me.

'Put your baby to bed . . . plea-se,' I whispered.

He did. He undressed me, tucked me in, switched off the light, closed my door quietly and staggered all the way back to his room in town.

There was no rehearsal the next day. Our manager knew that after a first-night celebration the actors were better left alone to cure their hangovers. This way he could count on them to be fit for the night's performance. I slept till Werner knocked on my window at noon.

'How's your head?' He greeted me.

'Not bad . . . not as bad as I deserve.'

'Careful, you are getting used to boozing,' he shook a finger at me.

I cooked a substantial lunch for us on the hot plate. We ate – and went back to bed and made love.

Chapter 16

'Annabel, here you are! I've been looking for you! Intermission is over, you are on in two minutes!' George, our prop man/stage manager, pulled me away from the sow and her twelve piglets, out of the stable, across the barnyard towards the stage. I heard my cue as soon as he opened the door. I lifted the long skirt of my gown and looked at my shoes. They were covered in muck – pig muck!

'Out,' George whispered.

My partners had started to improvise. 'I can see Dorothea approaching – I believe she got lost in the maze, the poor thing.'

I stepped into the scene. Our jolly manager, who played my father, embraced me – and immediately drew back.

'You stink,' he whispered between his teeth, 'don't come close . . . I'm afraid my daughter has a cold and has to keep her distance,' he said out loud. He was good at improvising, had to be. He often forgot his lines. It never diminished his performance – he was born to act.

'Annabel, stay away from the pigsty,' he grabbed me as soon as the curtain had come down. 'I'm sure the peasants of this community are used to the smell you are emanating – but have mercy with the delicate noses of your colleagues, please.' He pointed to his bulbous nose, a protuberance as big as a turnip.

The next time we performed in that farm community, one of the barn cats had kittens. I spent the entire intermission playing with the sweet little fur balls. I checked in with the pigs only briefly. Amazing how they had grown in just three weeks!

I felt as snug as a bug in a silk cocoon. My dream of becoming a famous actress was fading fast. I hardly ever practiced my voice exercises now, and my centre had quite simply dropped into that hidden, secret area of carnal pleasure. Poor Madame Cloutot! One of her few ardent students, Annabel Lambert, had finally slipped through her manipulating fingers. After a major role, I was satisfied to be given a small part in the next production. It meant less work, less responsibility – more time to cook a good meal on our hot plate and cuddle in bed with Werner. I discovered my creativity. In no time I had conjured a kitchen nook in my room. Our cooking equipment expanded from our raids on the only second-hand store in town, and from generous donations by our prop man. A gourmet chef would have been able to whip up his fabulous creations in my sanctum.

It wasn't just our meals that became more elaborate. My after-lunch embraces with Werner expanded too. I lost my inhibitions and became a brave amazon of love. I dared to touch my lover's erect penis – with one finger.

'You can take it in your hand,' Werner said. 'It won't bite you.' I did, with mixed feelings. It felt so alive! Werner had no problem touching me, he knew the right place, and he did it slowly and thoroughly. He never stopped until I was swept away into total oblivion. What an experience – what bliss! I was in awe of the wondrous workings of my body – how it was able to create and release this all-consuming energy.

Sometimes I wanted my love to stay longer inside me – I was amazed how nature had fitted our parts, how perfectly they came together. He was always finished fast because he had to withdraw to avoid pregnancy. I was thankful for that. I couldn't have coped with fretting about my period every month! We soon developed a satisfactory system – we took turns having orgasms. I never had to remind my lover whose turn it was.

One afternoon the doorbell rang while we were in the middle of 'the act'. I knew my young bride wasn't in and I certainly wasn't going to answer the door. The bell rang again – and again – longer each time, harder and more urgently each time. We moved apart.

'I'm sure I know who it is,' Werner whispered. 'Remember, Remus had a sore throat this morning. I bet he's lost his voice. Our jolly manager is out there. He's come to tell me I'll have to take over tonight.'

'No way, you couldn't possibly learn all the lines – and who would do your part?' I gasped.

'Anybody could do my few lines – but you are right, there's no way I could learn Remus' part. He's on in every act!'

We snuggled down under the covers and kept very still.

BOOM, BOOM, a knock at my window! The manager's big head rose up behind the glass. We slid to the edge of the bed and squeezed ourselves against the wall. I peered through a tiny gap between our improvised kitchen shelf, which covered half of the bed from view, and the wall. The jolly man pressed his face against the window-pane, cupped his hands around his eyes and tried to look in. He didn't appear jolly at all. We knew we were safe in our corner; nevertheless we pulled the covers over our heads, just in case. We were shivering and giggling at the same time. Our tormentor kept banging and banging. Was the window tightly locked? Was he going to break it? It was impossible now, after this length of time, to give ourselves away. He would have a high old time telling the entire company that he had found us in bed, so deeply entangled we didn't hear him pound on the window for ten minutes. We stayed motionless under the comforter. Two more angry blows - and quiet. I dared to peek out from under the cover. Gone! We heard his car start up. Gone!

When a couple of hours later we arrived together at the bus, he greeted us with a shout. 'Where the hell have you been, Werner? I went to your room, I drove to Annabel's, I bet you two were inside, I bet you were . . .'

'Oh no, how can you think that?' I answered in the softest of voices, 'we were out walking . . . back in the forest . . . we often do. Good for the lungs, you know.'

'Good acting! You should take it up professionally. Now I'm stuck acting as a young hero! Who is going to believe that?'

'I will, because you are a brilliant actor.'

'Smooth, girl,' he grinned, 'really smooth.'

My silk cocoon was ripped apart with a violence that made me tumble down into feelings I had never expected to be capable of. My darling Papa, no, no more darling, announced in a letter that my stepmother was pregnant! Pregnant at the age of forty! Can you think of anything more unsuitable, more disgusting? Who had babies at that age? My father was fifty-four and a grandfather! Oh, those stepmothers! The Brothers Grimm had known. They knew what devious creatures they were! I should have seen it coming. The kindness she had shown me – just a front. Like the rosy-cheeked apple SnowWhite was coaxed to bite into by her devious witch stepmother: 'Bite into it, my beauty' – and you are dead! I'm sure Hänsel and Gretel's stepmother sent the children into the forest to get lost because she was pregnant. Out with the old and in with the new! Oh, my poor Papa, how she had tricked you! I knew he didn't want another child. After the hard years of war and his responsibilities as a single father, he was looking forward to a quiet retirement. He had made sure there wouldn't be another baby. One day, while nosing around in their bedroom, I had found a packet of 'raincoats' in his bedside table. So how could she have become pregnant? – Ahaaa . . . she had secretly pricked the thing with a needle! Like the bad fairy had pricked Sleeping Beauty's finger and transported her out of the picture forever – or at least for a few hundred years.

I spat my anger at Werner when he returned from rehearsal. He listened with his usual patience – which only increased my fury. I wanted to scream SHIT at least half a dozen times, but he took me into his arms and kissed me gently on the forehead.

'Forget your conspiracy theory, Schatzi – those safes aren't guaranteed for safety. And forget the age thing. Charlie Chaplin is producing a whole clan, and he's what? Eighty?'

'Easy for you to joke about, you aren't the baby in your family.'

'Where does this remark come from?' Werner's quizzical expression disturbed me. Where did it come from? Did I, deep in my heart, still identify myself as my father's little princess? Had my love for Werner not frayed the cord that tied me to my daddy? Was he, Werner, not enough for me?

Not enough – that's what the Hawk had told me. We had celebrated the premiere performance of another play he had directed and I had starred in. A delightful musical comedy – chosen to soften the hearts and minds of our peasant clientele. *The Winter's Tale* was next – a real challenge! It wasn't only a Shakespeare play, but an unknown one as well. Our comedy had been a huge success because of the music, a rare treat. The songs were light and hummable and the audience felt pampered. When it was over, I stood in the wings and thanked the good fairy for letting me get away with it – nobody had booed down my singing! Werner, who could read music, had tried to rehearse some of the tunes with me prior to meeting the voice coach. He'd soon given up. 'Sorry Schatzi, I can't help you. You are off key, most of the time.'

'What are you talking about?' I had yelled. 'I have inherited my musicality from my Papa. You should hear him sing in the bath, whole opera arias, he could have been on stage with his voice, the neighbours have told him. You're just jealous they didn't cast you as my lover!' I wasn't going to let him put a curse on my voice.

At my first rehearsal with the singing coach, the man had hit the ivories, and I sang, loud, happy, confident. He didn't interrupt me. At the end I smiled at him and waited for praise.

'That was very good, Fräulein Lambert,' the coach said thoughtfully, 'but I think it will improve the song if you speak the words on the music – make it more into a chanson, like Marlene Dietrich does it . . . yes, you'll come across real sexy that way.'

'Ouch,' Werner said when I told him. 'He found you out. Do you believe me now that you can't hold a tune?' I hated him!

The morning after the first performance of our musical treat, my landlady caught me in the hall. I was in the habit of giving her free tickets.

'What a lovely little show,' she told me. 'I so enjoyed the music. And you looked so pretty! But you didn't really sing . . . did you now.' Darn!

Back to the Hawk and our first night party. As usual he was not holding back on his alcohol consumption, and I had imbibed freely as well. He became all gooey-eyed, took my hand, and without slurring his words told me that Werner wasn't enough for me. 'He's too kind, too soft, too accommodating for you. You'll soon get bored with him. You are of the wild kind, could be – you need someone who cracks the whip once in a while, who challenges you. Remember, Annabel, I told you first.' Good old Hawk – he knew more about me than I did.

Chapter 17

The *Winter's Tale* forced our manager to dig deep into his treasure chest, an action he could only bear by increasing his consumption of beer after our performance. 'Why are there so many bodies in every Shakespeare play? So many men?' He grumbled. He was forced to hire two male guests and one female. I was cast as the young lost daughter Perdita – and as her twelve-year-old brother! 'You've got to be joking,' I told our jolly manager. 'Not in the least, Fräulein Lambert. It works out beautifully. The boy is only on in the beginning, and Perdita appears for the first time in act four. You'll have all the time in the world to change.'

And change I did, because my protestations were half-hearted. The fairy tale mystery of the transformation intrigued me – and I felt flattered to be regarded as looking sufficiently young and innocent to portray a twelve- year-old boy. It was reassuring to know my intensive sex life hadn't tarnished my image.

At the first dress rehearsal the entire cast complimented me on my appearance. I looked so sweet, the women said, and they weren't in the habit of complimenting me. My costume consisted of white leggings, calf-high leather boots, a pair of those puffy little shorts with vertical gold stripes, a red brocade jacket with gold braiding, and one of those pancake caps with a feather up one side. My modest breasts were flattened by a girdle-like garment, and my long hair was tucked under my cap. Our noble old man, who was directing the tale, took me aside. 'You look utterly convincing, Annabel . . . your lean little figure . . . and what's more important, you have this child-like purity. If you like we'll keep the casting a secret . . . let's see if the audience can figure it out.' He squeezed my hand and chuckled.

As the noble old man had promised, my double casting wasn't mentioned in the program. Did the audience make the connection? My landlady certainly didn't. 'Where did they find that boy?' she asked me. 'He sure looked a lot like you. You really could have been brother and sister.' I smiled at her – the hammered-into-stone smile of a sphinx.

Florizel, the young prince who falls in love with Perdita, was played by one of the hired guests. It made me realize that Werner had never been cast in a leading role, and maybe never would. He was a supporting actor, not good-looking enough, and his voice not strong enough for a leading man. Thomas was good-looking, talented, charming, and ideal as a young lover. He reminded me in his boyish appearance and temper of my first love, Daniel, at the school in Berlin. One night, when exiting our scene, he gave me 'the look'. It struck me like lightening! Scary! What if I weren't involved with Werner, would we become lovers? Would I want to be loved by him? Oh, how could I deny it! Just to look into his eyes made my blood simmer.

'You seem to be giggling a lot together, you and Thomas,' Werner remarked after one of our performances.

'No need to worry, he's married. I would never get involved with a married man, never! It can only end in disaster . . . and I love you, don't I, my darling?' I had never said to him, I love you. It didn't seem necessary. It was obvious to everybody that we were in love. So how was it possible that Thomas excited me – made my heart go thump, thump – loud and clear?

The second I picked the envelope off the dresser in the hall, I had an uneasy feeling. I tore it open and my uneasiness turned into shock. For a moment I wanted to crumple up the letter, throw it into the waste bin and burn it – pretend it had never arrived. IT'S A GIRL, my stepmother had written in capital letters on the top of the page, and with coloured pencils she had fashioned a border of hearts and flowers around it. A girl! It hadn't occurred to me till that moment how a girl baby would change my life, my life with my darling Papa. Darling Papa and his little princess! Gone, finished, erased, torn out of the family album! No more princess, no longer baby daughter! Demoted to the rank of an understudy. All attention, all care from now on would go to the new baby girl. My Papa would hold her and rock her and coo to her and she would be so cute, so small, so helpless. He would love her as dearly as he once loved me. I stood there in the hall, in the darkness, and I felt the fear of the baby bird as it is being kicked out of its own nest by a cuckoo chick.

That night, sitting beside me on the bus, Werner was perplexed about the affection I poured on him. 'I like it when you are so loving,' he said. 'What have I done to deserve it?'

'You are here and you are mine, mine alone,' I whispered into his ear.

Our first season was coming to an end. We were both hired for a second year. We hadn't applied at other theatres, as our agents had suggested, because a move would most certainly mean separation – unthinkable. I decided not to spend my time off at my father's house. I knew our special bond was broken, and I wasn't keen on meeting my replacement.

I accepted an invitation from Werner's parents in Bavaria so we could be together. 'But not in bed,' Werner warned. 'My mother wouldn't tolerate it.'

We decided to buy a couple of mopeds, glorified motorized bicycles that looked like the popular Italian-made Vespa – from a distance. Thanks to my economic skills, Werner called me a miser, we could offer the dealer a substantial down payment, and he granted us credit for the rest. He knew we were employed for the next season.

Our mopeds were powder blue with dark blue trim, built by BMW. When first I mounted mine, I felt like I was taking a new Mercedes 300 SL for a spin. In contrast to the automobile, no permit was required to operate our little machines – their top speed was thirty kilometres. I had no problem starting the motor – to make it move was a challenge! You had to let the clutch out ever so slowly or bloop – it died! Werner got the hang of it in a jiffy, and he showed his characteristic patience with me. As soon as he noticed I was lagging behind, he would stop and wait for me. I couldn't ever wait for him. Who knows how long it would take me to get into gear again!

After three days of practice we were ready for the trip all across Germany – northwest to southeast. We worked out a route on secondary roads. No mopeds allowed on the *Autobahn*, thank God. We bought side pockets to hang over the rear wheels and squashed knapsacks and blankets onto the carrier. When I attempted to mount, the whole thing toppled over. 'Unbalanced load,' Werner commented. 'Maybe you want to leave the cooking utensils behind. There'll be plenty of inns along the way.

'But eating out is expensive,' I protested. When my moped toppled over a second time, I gave in. No pots or pans! I threw all my careful financial calculations out the window. I was ready to live the carefree life.

Chapter 18

Oh what a feeling! We had left early and sure enough, the road was ours. I sat on my own brand new machine, the wind blew in my face, and the fresh air sharpened my senses. Meadows dotted with grazing cows lined the sides of the road, thatched farm cottages peeked out of the morning mist, and the odd windmill turned slowly in a gentle breeze. And at the speed we were going there was plenty of time to take it all in. The best part though was Werner beside me, or in front, or behind – always there, always close. What joy! I wouldn't have wanted to change places with the Queen of England or the Maharani of Jalapur!

At dusk, we booked ourselves into guesthouses as Herr and Frau Werner Helwig. Starched white sheets, puffy eiderdowns, together all night! Our sore bums didn't prevent us from making love. Squeak, squeak, went the bedsprings – we didn't care. We were a married couple. We had the right to make the springs squeak!

The weather was dry and warm through the entire trip. Somebody up there loves us, Werner commented. Our faces got sunburned. I laughed at Werner who tried to attach a chestnut leaf to his nose. The wind just loved his efforts! We learned to plaster our faces and hands with *Nivea* lotion.

Our chosen route along the Rhine turned out to be flat and picturesque. Castles, the Lorelei Rock, the terraced vineyards and small villages squeezed into the banks of the river, thrilled me. On the water, white cruise ships loaded with tourists ploughed their way south or north, and an endless line of barges, sitting deep in the water, made their way slowly toward their destinations. We waved at children who played on the decks while their mothers were hanging up laundry. It was like watching a movie.

Unfortunately we weren't able to circumvent cities altogether, and cities had traffic lights. My problem: I couldn't get the first gear in fast enough when the light turned green. I hated being in line at a traffic light on a two-lane street. I knew I wouldn't get away when the light changed. A horn would sound behind me – let the clutch out slowly, slowly – bloop – I had killed the motor. Get off the saddle, jump on the right peddle – the motor is running again – more horns, loud and long – release slowly, slowly – I'm moving, moving! Now brakes are squealing – a man is hanging out of his car window shouting 'Are you blind!' I'm stopped again – in the middle of the intersection. Cars on my left and on my right – waiting. A voice 'Push off, push that mosquito out of the way!' Good idea! I smile to the right and to the left and push my powder blue BMW built machine out of the intersection. Werner is waiting for me.

'Schatzi, you need to be more careful! Didn't you notice that the light had changed?'

'No – I tried to get moving! How can I look at the light at the same time?'

'Soon as we are out of town let's stop and look at the map. There's got to be a way to avoid Offenbach – for your safety and my nerves.'

Gradually, the territory became more mountainous - beautiful to look at, but hard on our motors. Now our top speed was twenty, then ten kilometres. Finally we were crawling up mountains, and flying down into valleys, motor off, legs up on the handlebars, saving fuel. Crawling up became tiring, boring - my eyes wanted to close, close . . .

'Annabel, Annaaaaaaa . . . what are you doing? Pull over to the side – you are in the middle of the road!' Werner's voice – where was it coming from? A car horn - blurr, blurr - it startled me. I was awake in an instant. I pulled over.

'Stay home you stupid bitch . . .' the driver of a car shouted as he sped past me. Werner had caught up to me.

'Did you actually fall asleep? I couldn't get to you, I wasn't able to go any faster.'

'I think my motor is a little peppier than yours – or maybe it's the weight. Maybe you should lose a few pounds if you want to keep up with me.'

Even my peppy machine gave up on the steeper hills. We had to get off and push. Nasty comments from the cars and motorcycles that passed us.

'You can ride with me Liebling – forget the boy with the sewing machine!'

'Get lost, you stupid shit head!'

'Be careful, Schatzi,' Werner warned, 'we are in Bavaria now. The young men here like nothing better than a good fight. For these rowdies a great night at the pub means three guys in hospital, the place crashed up, and several arrests by the police.' I limited my outbursts to pointing a finger to my head.

The night before we reached our destination, Werner told me, in more detail, the situation at his home. His father had been unfaithful with a woman he had met on his daily commute to work. His mother, furious about the affair, had surprised them one day at the railroad station and hit the woman with her umbrella. The stationmaster had got involved and the story soon spread through the entire village. Nevertheless his parents kept living under the same roof – just didn't talk to each other.

'Why don't they get a divorce? I'm sure both of their lives would improve.'

'With my mother it's the religious thing. She's a devout Catholic. Marriage is a sacrament – if you break it you are condemned to burn in hell for all eternity. She will never agree to a divorce.'

'Marriage, hell and religion, they seem to have something in common,' I joked. Werner didn't laugh.

When our destination loomed ahead, we decided to take a rest and make love for the last time in – three weeks? We parked the mopeds in a ditch beside the road, took a couple of blankets and walked deep into a meadow where the grass was as high as our shoulders. We discovered a tiny brook that went gurgling on its way, with buttercups lining the banks. A lovely spot! We knelt down on the ground and looked around. We were covered from all sides. We spread the blanket and went on with what we had come for.

Swish, swish – the wind? There wasn't any. A cap appeared over the top of the grass, moving towards us.

'Get off me, fast – there's someone walking!'

My lover rolled off me just as a young man stepped out of the high grass. I grabbed the extra blanket and pulled it over the parts below the belt.

'Werner Helwig, is it you? How long have you been back in town?'

Werner had sat up instantly. I thanked the good fairy. We had stripped only where necessary for our purpose.

'Oh, we just got in, Heinz,' Werner mumbled. Beads of sweat were forming on his forehead.

'How is the acting business? You still doing it?' Heinz crouched down and took a fishing rod off his shoulder. He was ready to catch up on any new development in Werner's life.

'This your girlfriend?' He pointed at me.

'This is Annabel Lambert,' Werner hurried to say. 'Annabel meet my school-mate Heinz Untermeier.'

'Glad to make your acquaintance,' I lied. Please, shove off! My bare bum is getting damp!

'I met your mother the other day,' Heinz went on, 'she told me you are employed in a town in the north. How can you stand it so far away from home?' Judging by his heavy Bavarian accent, and his ignorance of the situation, I was sure Heinz had been born in this little town and he would die there.

'I like it in Cleves,' Werner said. When he didn't volunteer any further information, Heinz got the message. He rose.

'Maybe we can go for a beer one day,' he muttered. 'Adios!'

We looked at each other and clamped our hands over our mouths. When Heinz was out of earshot we broke loose. We hollered and screeched with laughter.

'Wait till he tells your mother,' I teased.

'We better get to her first.' Werner quickly folded up the blankets.

'Heinz is naive enough to go into details about the way he met us.'

Chapter 19

Our Bavarian vacation was a disaster. An aura of doom and gloom seemed to surround Werner's mother. His father, in contrast, was cheerful and pleasant. 'He's the one who had the fun,' Werner reminded me. 'My mother wasn't always so sullen, believe me.' Still, I couldn't relax in her presence. I was sure she suspected our illegitimate sex life and disapproved of me. She was determined to put a halt to it as long as we stayed in her cave, I mean under her roof. If we expressed the desire to go for a walk, Frau Helwig insisted on accompanying us. She could neither walk fast nor far – it was agony to have her around. I liked to skip and run, and explore the woods by climbing on rocks or balancing on fallen trees. With her I had to walk like an old lady out for a Sunday stroll. My mood took another dive when Werner's sister came to visit – her two small children in tow. Now the house, small to begin with, was overflowing. How do you find space for five adults and two children in a two-bedroom house? On account of the affair, Frau Helwig had forever banned her husband from their bedroom. He was in the doghouse, literally. He slept in a closet-size room in the cellar. At our arrival, I had been given the spare bedroom, while Werner had to share his mother's space. I visualized her as a fire-breathing dragon guarding the cave where she was sheltering her son – protecting him from the sin of fornication. When her daughter and the children joined us, the dragon came up with the following arrangement: I had to share the room with Werner's sister and the baby child, while the older offspring was bedded on the sofa in the living room. Any nocturnal encounters, however daring and quiet, were out of the question. We suffered – Werner more than I. He was used to having sexual relief every other day, now there was none. He was not a do-it-yourselfer: his altar boy education had left him with a full-blown complex in regard to that practice. Needless to say, as the days passed, he got desperate. Finally he came up with a plan. 'I'll tell my mother you are going to wash my hair in the bathroom. Maybe we can . . .'

We locked the door ever so carefully making sure no click could be heard. I started the shampoo. I worked the lather on Werner's head with one hand and his penis with the other. He didn't need long. 'Quiet,' I hissed when he started to groan, 'turn up the water.' My intense work had aroused me too – only this time I didn't get a turn.

'Are you finished Uncle Werner?' The voice of his niece filtered through the door. 'I have to go pee.'

'Yes, I'm finished.' Werner zipped up his fly. I unlocked the door with the skill of a professional safe cracker, and pulled it open. His niece found her uncle rubbing his head with a towel.

Oh, I knew she would bring it up – I was sure of it. I had been waiting with bated breath for her question, and had rehearsed a variety of answers in my head. The moment came after a mid-day meal I had cooked for us. I was tired of her poor cooking – she had lost all interest in her *Hausfrau* duties, and her meals were a prime example. As much as I resented my stepmother, I had to admit it: she was a good cook. I'd been her most eager student – I felt confident at the stove. Now everybody was praising my effort: new potatoes, asparagus with a cheese sauce, and veal cutlets. Chocolate pudding topped with whipped cream and crowned by a perfect sweet cherry, for dessert. The kids were smacking their lips.

'You can cook a good meal, Annabel,' Frau Helwig started her attack. 'Do you enjoy housework?' Before I had time to answer the fire-breathing dragon spewed its vitriolic question at me:

'When are you and Werner going to get married?'

I was prepared. I chose the least insulting and least committing answer.

'Right now we have one more year in Cleves, but after that, who knows? There are very few married couples in the same company. It's regarded as fostering conflict . . . favouritism and such . . . so I'm afraid we might have to wait.'

'Once Werner has a lucrative contract, and I'm sure he will when he starts applying at bigger companies, you might want to give up acting and find a job in an office. Nothing would stand in the way of your marriage then.'

Patience, patience, bite your lip! Her fire can't burn you.

'Ja, maybe . . .' I looked at Werner. His eyes pleaded with me not to blow my top. 'Maybe . . .' I repeated – a fake smile on my face. I have to get away from here, soon, was my next thought. I was afraid I would use my sword to fight the dragon next time.

Home started to look more comfortable by the hour. And to tell the truth, I didn't have a choice. Home was the only place I could escape to. Werner understood my decision. 'If I don't have you around, I'll be able to bear my celibacy with greater ease. When the spark is gone, the fire will die out,' he joked.

I arrived home with a heart full of sadness, guilt and unexpected joy when my Papa took me in his arms. There was so much warmth and understanding in his eyes – I couldn't play the part of a neglected, unwelcome daughter as I had intended. And despite my childish, jealous behaviour, the good fairy hadn't abandoned me. My stepmother was going to be out of the picture for a while. She was travelling to Berlin to be with her mother. A minor stroke had put Oma into the hospital. Since

Mama was nursing, she had to take the baby with her. A stroke, poor Oma! Maybe she had overdone her sexual escapades? Poor Oma! I felt sorry for her, but I couldn't help being delighted to have my darling Papa all to myself.

Over the next few days it became clear that our relationship could never be the same again – the way it had been before my half sister was born. Papa never asked me how deeply I was involved with Werner. I avoided talking about my successor – how hurt I felt about being kicked off my pedestal. I didn't want to make him sad. So we lived alongside each other like an old couple, married for a hundred years. We knew we loved each other – but that special affection, that joy I had felt in his presence, was now gone.

Chapter 20

A second season in Cleves! Werner and I continued playing house as before – a change in the ensemble didn't disrupt our idyllic existence. Our two young women had moved on and their replacements, when I saw their pictures on the bulletin board, made my heart sink. They looked gorgeous! One was downright beautiful, the other had a smile to kill for. Both looked young, very young.

'Don't worry, our noble old man loves you. He'll make sure you get your parts,' Werner consoled me. He was referring to a scene that had left no doubt about our senior director's affections for me. We had been rehearsing a comedy in Friesian dialect, a bribe to keep our peasant clientele happy and on board. I was cast as the daughter of a wealthy farmer, and Werner was Johann, a poor farm hand I fallen in love with. After the first run-through the old man stepped onto the stage, notepad in hand.

'Annabelchen', he said, 'I couldn't quite hear you when you were whispering to Johann in the second act.' And in a strict tone of voice, 'Werner, you are to turn away from her – as I told you before. Turn! Right away – not half an hour later!' The assembled cast looked at me – I smiled. I loved the old man too. On our way to my room Werner kept teasing me.

'Annabelchen, do you think you can cook some lunch for us when we get home?' He sounded more amused than jealous. He knew neither our director nor I would ever act on our feelings for each other. Only in my dreams did I find myself in the old man's arms, feeling loved and safe.

We met the new company members in person at our first rehearsal for the new season. My anxiety meter dropped.

'What a fool I am, what a fool!' I whispered to Werner. 'I was afraid of the two new women because of their pictures! They look nothing like it! The beautiful one has an ordinary face, pretty maybe – and she is so short! I think the other is even less attractive, although she has a better figure. I should have remembered my stunning pictures! Were you fooled by them?'

'No, I liked you right away. I thought you looked lovely.'

'You always say the right thing. I'm glad you are mine, Liebling.'

It turned out that the two new females were amiable, friendly creatures with limited ambitions. One soon submitted to the Hawk's rigorous, no-nonsense advances, which didn't prevent him from giving me the eye occasionally. In a weird way, I liked it that he still wanted me. The other girl stayed faithful to a faraway boyfriend. I made no effort to get to know them better. I had Werner – he was all I needed.

As I had learned in my relationship with my father, nothing is perfect for long. Werner and I had to apply at other theatres in larger cities. More than two years in the province looked like giving up on a career. Our agents went to work. After a couple of unsuccessful auditions, I was hired at the *Landestheater* in Lippburg, a medium-sized company, a step up. Was I jubilant? No, furious! There was no position for Werner in Lippburg and that meant separation.

'Shit!' I screamed. 'Shit, shit, shit! What are we going to do? I need you! I can't be by myself . . . all alone in the woods!'

'You have to go, that's for certain. Unless you want to give up acting?' I shook my head. 'I didn't think so. If our love is strong enough, it will last for . . .' My sniggering interrupted him.

'What play are these noble words from – love strong enough? Really, you can be so pathetic, I mean . . . poetic, at times.'

'And you better cut down on your swearing! One SHIT spoken with the right emphasis is enough.'

Werner decided to move to Düsseldorf where a company called *Boulevard Theater*, a private enterprise, had offered him a part – and maybe more in the future. There was also the chance to get in with other theatre companies: there were several in the area.

'I can hop on my moped and be with you in Lippburg in three hours. I'm sure we can make it work.' Werner's face contradicted his words. He looked positively miserable.

Saying goodbye to our noble director made me snivel. I was going to lose the security his love had provided for me. Without him, I would be exposed to all the favouritisms and intrigues every theatre company was prone to. How was I going to manage without his protection? I felt tears flooding my eyes when he took my hand and held it in both of his. 'I believe in you, Annabelchen,' he said. 'You'll be alright.' My tears started to roll. I was sure the artistic director in Lippburg would never call me Annabelchen - nobody there would.

I spent the time between the end of my old contract and the beginning of the new at home. Poor Papa, his loving wife had found another love, another passion. My stepmama's emotional life circled solely and without any sign of guilt around her new daughter, her own flesh and blood. She clucked over her like a hen over her chicks, cluck, cluck, cluck, day and night. She had gone so far as to move into the baby's room. My Papa said out of consideration for him – ha, she had another agenda! She was no longer interested in sex with him, the witch. I despised her for the trick she played on him – poor Papa. I couldn't give him what he needed – he wanted *her* attention. Stepmothers - had there ever been one who brought happiness? Not in a fairy tale *I* know of.

Chapter 21

1958 - 1959

The rain was pouring down in sheets when my train arrived in Lippburg. Stepping onto the platform, I opened my umbrella. With one colossal gust the wind turned it inside out and left me, swearing under my breath, exposed to the downpour. As a child I used to dance under such a warm summer rain pretending Mother Holle was raining her gold onto me. Now I felt like I was being punished with a downpour of tar. What a start! I picked up my suitcase, tottered under its weight, and stepped into a puddle. Shit! My new shoes, a gift from my poor Papa, ruined. I couldn't afford a taxi but – this was an emergency. I waited in the damp, smoke-infested waiting room for half an hour. The few taxis that operated in this town were busy, the stationmaster pointed out, due to the weather. I had guessed that myself. 'Patience Fräulein,' he said, 'it won't be much longer.'

The taxi driver, when one finally arrived, was short-tempered. 'I've been driving non-stop since six o'clock, hope you don't have to go far. My wife is waiting with my lunch.' I gave him my address. 'That's right in the middle of town. You could have walked.' I shot him a hostile glance. ' If it wasn't for the suitcase,' he mumbled. After a five-minute drive he turned into a narrow cobblestone street and stopped in front of a half-timbered house. Its façade bulged under the weight of the ages – it looked like it wouldn't survive the present century. The taxi driver developed some human compassion and carried my suitcase to the front door. 'You'll have to get used to the church bell,' he muttered. 'Strikes every hour, day and night.' He pointed to a huge, squat stone church and its square tower, right across the street, with a graveyard off to one side. Another bad omen? I remembered the cemetery at Oma's in Berlin, where Annabel was buried. Annabel, whose name I had adopted. I had promised her I would fulfil my dream, a chance not given to her. Be strong, I told myself. This is the town where you'll make your way! Forget cozy, delightful afternoons of pleasure. Your job, your career is all that matters for you here.

The wooden front door stood ajar. A cloud of steam floated towards me as I proceeded deeper into the dimly lit corridor. A smell of boiling laundry reminded me of Mondays at home – wash day. A youngish woman, hair covered by a scarf, materialized out of the cloud. She dried her hand on her apron, then reached out and shook mine.

'You must be Fräulein Lambert,' she said. 'We have been expecting you. I hope you'll like the room . . . Peter!' she called into the steam behind her, 'come and help our new boarder upstairs.' A tall boy with a head of wild curls became visible. 'This is my son,' my new hostess said. 'He's a good worker, helps me in the laundry. Hope you don't mind the damp - you won't notice up on the third floor. I started the business when my husband didn't come back from the war. With Peter's help and a half-day girl it's a profitable enterprise now – and you shall profit too. Your washing is included in the rental. Does that sound fair?'

'Very . . . thank you.' I was eager to get to my room and out of my wet clothes. Peter, showing off his strength, heaved my suitcase onto one shoulder and sprinted up the stairs, two steps at a time. He stopped on a landing, looked back over his free shoulder and pointed upward. I followed him, my feet making a squashing sound in my wet shoes. After climbing the third set of stairs, we arrived at the attic. Peter opened a door and deposited the case inside the room. He disappeared down the stairs as fast as he had climbed them. The room was bright, even on this dull day. Two windows allowed an unobstructed view of the church tower and the huge bell suspended in its peak. BONG . . . BONG! The walls of the room vibrated. I covered my ears. It was two o'clock. I sat down on the bed and let myself drop back – and banged my head on the slanted wall behind. SHIT! What's next? I shivered in my wet clothing. My throat felt tight. No, I wasn't going to cry! I swallowed hard once, twice, pulled off my clothes and crawled into bed. The mattress felt firm, no sagging; the eiderdown was puffy and too warm for late summer. Never mind, it felt so comfortable, so soothing. I pulled up my legs and curled myself into a ball. I thought of Werner and his embraces and his love for me . . . his love . . .

I met the full ensemble and the directors the next morning. I was ready to face them after a sleep of fourteen hours. The bong of the church bell had awoken me only once – at midnight, no wonder. I had met the head artistic director before, at my audition. He was a middle-aged, balding man with a beer belly – there was nothing of the artist about him. He might well have been an accountant like his wife, who worked in an office. In contrast, the second director met all the expectations one might have of an artistic personality. He was a short, very short, thin man with a freckled face, close-set blue eyes, and short-cropped red hair. He wore a shawl draped around his neck and a cold pipe in his mouth. Cold is what I felt when I was introduced to him. He briefly looked at me, mumbled something under his breath, then joined some of the actors who immediately flocked around him. They knew each other well. Some had worked for three years with him. In Cleves the Hawk had attacked me - this man ignored me. I soon learned that he was homosexual, which didn't prevent most of the actresses from buzzing around him like worker bees around the queen. Oh Cleves, what an easy, comfortable time I had left behind! Now I had to face competition. There was one actress of exactly my age, one, the young heroine, about five years older, and still another young woman, Hanna, who talked to me and confessed that she felt as lost as I did. The three older women I didn't have to fear. They were old enough to act as my mothers.

My first part was a take-over from my predecessor, who had moved up and away, and who had been extremely popular not only with all the males, but also with the women in the cast. How had she done it? Since I wasn't her, and was only given one run-through of this rather complicated production – a Spanish comedy, hailed as the oh-so artistically talented Queen Bee's masterpiece – my performance was criticized and clucked over by all involved. I'm sure I didn't do the part justice – I was preoccupied with trying to be at the right place at the right time and saying the right lines – I had no chance to get into the character. The Queen Bee felt betrayed, and further ignored me, if that was possible. I thanked the good fairy for other Cinderellas. Hanna, who felt as lost and unappreciated as I, became my friend. She reminded me of Donata, whose friendship had made my school days in Berlin bearable. I felt at home with Hanna. I knew I could trust her – in contrast to the young actress my age, Karin the Snooper. She had the nerve to show up uninvited at my place one morning.

'Just want to see how you are doing,' she greeted me, as she stepped into my room without being asked. 'I know you must be lonely. Too bad your boyfriend couldn't join you here . . . you must miss him terribly.' How did she know about

Werner's unsuccessful application? Was she in thick with the top boss, the ruler of the entire enterprise? She wasn't hooked up with anybody in particular, I had noticed, but hung around with a young homosexual actor they called Wolfie and the Queen Bee. She was also close with everybody else, including the stagehands. How did she do it? Try to be friends with her Annabel – talk about Werner, about Cleves, tell her how much you liked her last performance, pat her on the back! But I couldn't. I knew whatever I told her would make the round of the entire ensemble. It was safer to stick with the cinders in the kitchen – safer to share the warmth and compassion Hanna's friendship offered.

Chapter 22

If only I didn't feel so alone in the evenings when I had no performance! Oh Werner, you have spoiled me! I had to learn to live alone all over again. To forget my loneliness, I went for long walks. Lippburg, I had discovered, was huddled against the southern foot of the Teutoburg Forest, an area dotted with spa towns. From my laundry/landlady I learned that it had been a garrison town ruled by the Duke of Lippburg. His heirs still maintained a box in the theatre their father or grandfather had built in grandiose Greek style. My daily walk to work led me through a park with a pond in the centre, formerly the Duke's estate, now public and enjoyed by flocks of ducks, geese and a pair of swans. Watching the birds, I was able to forget my isolation. I envied the creatures their carefree existence, their total absorption in the task at hand – like pruning their feathers.

The Duke's theatre now served the surrounding smaller communities similar to the setup in Cleves, but here we only travelled to a couple of spa towns with each play. The majority of our audiences were bussed to us. Our travels to the spa towns were regarded as a special treat by the cast. There was time before the performance to walk in the well-kept gardens that surrounded the sanatoriums, and drink a glass or two of the healing waters – or listen to a late concert of the *Kurorchester*. I was glad I had Hanna at my side on these trips. The other members of the cast, familiar with the surroundings, would disappear in cliques to some popular inn. We were not invited to join them. Oh Werner, why couldn't you come to me? I poured out my heart to him in letters and got reassuring answers. Yes, he missed me, missed me terribly – but he couldn't join me. His show was a success. For a private enterprise, such as the *Boulevard Theater*, having an 'in demand' show is equivalent to hitting a gold mine. You keep digging. As word of mouth gets around, new people buy tickets and keep the house sold out. There was no chance for Werner to slip away. Phone calls were expensive, and miser that I was, I couldn't bear going into debt. So, the written word had to do.

'Annabel, Annabel let me in!' Hanna was standing on the street shouting up to my window. The front door was locked. My hostess was having her mid-day meal. I flew down the stairs.

'Have you looked at the board this morning? You are cast as Leonie in our next production. You, not Karin the Snooper! It's one of the leading parts – maybe not the lead, but leading . . .'

'To disaster if I don't pull it off!' I had hoped and prayed for that part - now that it was mine I felt scared.

'Who is directing?'

'Our family man with the beer belly. You have nothing to fear.'

'Who is my lover?' I asked a little too fast.

'Sweet Wolfie. He's a good actor, as you know, and he won't try to seduce you – so enjoy!'

I had hoped for Sebastian Schoen, the best-looking young man in the ensemble. I had met him briefly in the hall a couple of times, and I had watched him on stage. His handsomeness wasn't his only asset. He also had a beautiful voice, and the way he carried himself – I was sure Madame Cloutot would gush over him! He acted from the centre! The first time I saw him off-stage, he was engaged in an intense conversation with our artistic head with the beer belly. I don't know if he noticed me. The second time, Karin the Snoop was hanging on his arm. That time he smiled at me. At another of her uninvited visits, the Snoop hastened to tell me that Sebastian was married, and that his wife was a fashion model. Most of her assignments were in Düsseldorf, which explained her frequent absences. I had the suspicion the Snoop was using these absences to her advantage. I didn't blame her. What girl in her right mind wouldn't want to be with a man like Sebastian!

The play was a witty French comedy, and my part was exciting. I had to laugh in one scene, cry in another, flirt with one partner and reject another. My outfits, perfectly fitted by the costume department, were gorgeous. Sadly, the Beerbelly turned out to be one of the less gifted directors – more of a solid craftsman. His direction neither inspired nor challenged me. He said little and I became anxious. Had I found the right tone, the right body language? Was I acting from the centre? I missed Werner's input. I knew I could trust him. He wasn't afraid to call my bluff if my performance didn't convince him.

Hanna was the first to congratulate me after opening night.

'You looked lovely,' she said. 'Those dresses, the riding outfit – classy, you looked classy.'

The Queen Bee showed up at our first-night party. He looked at me and nodded. Did that mean he approved?

Sebastian Schoen drifted in after midnight. He and the rest of the ensemble had performed in one of the spa towns that night. When I got up to leave he suddenly appeared at my side.

'Congratulations,' he said. 'I liked your performance. You have an honesty . . .' he looked straight into my eyes and smiled. I felt my legs weaken. Too much booze . . .

'But you haven't seen the show . . .' I stuttered.

'I watched the dress rehearsal,' he said. 'Didn't you notice me?' That smile again. I shook my head and hurried towards the door. When I turned to wave goodbye to Hanna, he was still standing where I had left him, smiling.

'Fräulein Lambert,' a voice – and a knock at my door. 'Fräulein Lambert, are you awake?' I was now. I tried to raise my head but couldn't – too heavy.

'It's Peter,' the voice said. 'I got you the newspaper. The reporter liked your performance last night. I'll slide the paper through. You can read it for yourself.' Good, curly headed Peter. He was proud of having an actress live in his house. The times we had met accidentally in the corridor, he had blushed. I think he had a crush on me.

In the afternoon, at rehearsal for our next production, I noticed that my prestige had been raised a notch. The two mature actors in the cast, married to absent wives, started to flirt with me. The stage manager announced that I had a perfect arse. The riding costume! But my real breakthrough happened in a fairy tale – the customary Christmas production.

Snow-White and Rose-Red, a play based on the tale by the Brothers Grimm, had been chosen. No wicked stepmother in this one, just a wicked dwarf, who reminded me of the Queen Bee. The Snoop was cast as Rose-Red, and our young heroine as Snow-White. After three performances the heroine, greatly overworked, collapsed. I was asked to take over. I was thrilled – and scared. Undoubtedly I would be compared to our oh-so-popular leading lady. Never mind, I knew I had an advantage over her – I was better suited, and I took the part as seriously as any other – something my fellow actors teased me about. They thought acting in a fairy tale was a hoot. They improvised and tried to make each other laugh every chance they got. I refused to join their game because I loved playing for the children. Their oohs and aahs were spontaneous and honest. You couldn't fool them. To my delight they picked up on the prince's insincere performance. When, at the end of the story, he asked Snow-White to marry him, a little voice shouted 'Say no, nooo! Not him!' He wasn't laughing then.

The Queen Bee, who had directed the tale, spoke his first words to me after a couple of performances. The young stage manager, one of his devoted worker bees, stopped me after my third performance. 'Yeah,' he said, 'you really come across as a completely innocent girl. The kids can relate to you. Well done, Annabel.'

'You're much better than our heroine,' Hanna told me. 'She was too old and too sophisticated for the part. They should have cast you in the first place – it's your genre.' My prestige in the company was raised another notch. My nose was above water level now. I could breathe more freely.

Chapter 23

It was my first Christmas away from home. There wasn't enough time to make the trip because *Snow-White and Rose-Red* ran on Christmas Eve, in the afternoon, and again on Boxing Day. I had so hoped my Papa would come to one of the earlier performances. I was sure watching me as Snow-White would have given him pleasure - made him feel proud. But because the baby was teething, he hadn't made the trip. He couldn't leave my stepmother alone with all the crying at night. My needs didn't count anymore! Now that his wife had her own offspring, I could imagine her plotting on how to get rid of me. Maybe send me into the deep forest to be eaten by wild beasts? Hah - that wouldn't work. There were no more wild beasts around. The only wild thing was my imagination - and I loved to unleash it.

My hostess, sensing my abandonment, invited me to the customary Christmas Eve celebration. There were two people present whom I hadn't met: her mother and her male friend. I was glad she had a man in her life. Peter was happy to have me close – he had a permanent blush on his face. After his mother had presented him with his present, his first dark suit complete with white shirt and silk tie, he handed me a tiny parcel wrapped in gold paper, and tied with a big red ribbon. It turned out to be a jewellery box. I was stunned to find, bedded on a tiny damask cushion, a silver ring bearing a couple of tiny diamonds. 'Oh Peter!' I gasped, 'that's too much!'

'Will you wear it please?' Peter's cheeks had turned a still darker red.

'I sure will, Peter, thank you very much.' I kissed him on the cheek. He maintained a dreamlike expression on his face for the whole night. I was glad I had made somebody happy.

The day after New Year's, it was my turn to be flushed with happiness. A telegram from Werner announced his coming. His play had finally closed. He would be with me the next day. In only a few hours, he would hold me in his arms!

When he walked along the platform towards me, I noticed that he needed a haircut; the longer hair didn't suit him. He had gained weight – too many beers, I was sure. But it felt good when he took me in his arms and kissed me.

To make it easier for my landlady to accept Werner in my room overnight, neither of us had the money for a room in a *Gasthaus* for a full week, we told her we were engaged. It worked.

The morning after Werner's arrival, the Snoop came snooping.

'Oh, I'm sorry,' she exclaimed, 'I didn't know you had a visitor!' We were still in bed. It had been a long night – talking and making love.

'Is this Werner?' She hardly gave him a chance to pull on a pair of pants. I made the introductions. She smiled at him.

'I have to tell you, Werner, we all like Annabel. She is such a sincere person.'

The Snoop wasn't down the three flights of stairs when we could no longer hold back our laughter. I got caught in a proper laugh attack – it felt so good to laugh out loud and to be joined by someone who felt the same way, who enjoyed the same kind of humour.

'Come here, you sincere person,' Werner sputtered, 'you were smart not to get intimate with her. She strikes me as the typical career actress. From what you have told me in your letters, she'll climb the ladder of success in a hurry.'

'What about me? How do you rate my chances for success?'

'I'm not sure . . . you aren't as ambitious . . . and you don't know how to schmooze. You are too honest . . . that's why I love you. You are not obsessed with your career. You like and enjoy so many other things. You go nuts over a stray dog or a cat . . . you talk to trees . . . you devour books . . . you put your heart into cooking a good meal . . . and your imagination is limitless! Oh I mustn't forget your most endearing feature:

You have no problem lying around here with me talking and making love for hours. I'm sure the Snoop is either doing her voice exercises now, or she's having morning coffee with the Queen Bee, pumping him discreetly about her next leading part.'

'You aren't obsessed either, if you were, you would be making the rounds in Düsseldorf, instead of making love to me. We are well matched.'

The next day Werner went to the barber and got a brush cut. It looked good on him. I made an appointment with our theatre photographer. She took a series of portraits, very professional looking, for a reasonable price. I liked one in particular – its only flaw was the presence of a fat vein snaking along part of his forehead. 'Too much sex,' Werner said. 'It does that to a man.'

'Oh you poor thing. I promise I'll stay away from you from now on.'

'Don't you dare, Schatzi,' he whispered. 'Don't you dare!'

Werner was gone, and the nights when I had no performance became a dark tunnel again with no light at the end. I was once again lost in the woods and no cozy cottage inhabited by seven quirky dwarves was waiting for me. I went to see a French film that everyone in our ensemble was raving about: *Fanfan la Tulipe*. I was enthralled by the light-hearted story, the flawless direction by Christian-Jaque, the well-cast supporting actors and the star – Gérard Philipe. I left the theatre with a smile on my face and Philipe in my heart. His fabulous looks, his boyish charm, and his wide-awake eyes had put a spell on me. That night, I fell asleep sitting behind him on his horse, holding him tightly around the waist, feeling strands of his dark hair caressing my face, as we are galloping through the delightful French countryside.

Happiness in reality arrived when I was cast as Adelheid, a loud-mouthed teenager who talks with a Berlin accent, in *The Beaver Coat* by Gerhart Hauptmann. What a quirky part! The accent came easily – I hadn't spent two years in Berlin for nothing, and for once, I didn't have to be all good and pure. Another lucky break was the presence of Sebastian Schoen, who had a minor part in the same play. His scene directly followed one of mine. During rehearsal we spent considerable time together waiting to be called on stage. Finally I got to know him. Although his looks were impressive – blond, blue eyes, medium height, a face suitable for playing any classical hero – he was also an intelligent, sensitive man. We talked about Rilke, his favourite poet, and Thomas Mann's *Der Zauberberg*, which I had started to read, but was finding hard to get through without skipping pages. The Snoop, faithful to her name, kept joining into our conversation whenever she got a chance. Once, while Sebastian was 'on' she hastened to tell me about his beautiful wife. 'She bought him the Vespa he's driving . . . for his birthday . . . she makes a lot of money with her modelling.'

Get lost, you jealous bitch, I would have liked to answer, and chum up with the Queen Bee and all your other pals! Oh, why couldn't I do it – why not let her have it! I had no trouble calling her a bitch in my head. Why couldn't I say it out loud? What was I afraid of?

Chapter 24

I was standing in the wings waiting for my entrance. Sebastian appeared at my side. We stood close and quiet, in the dark. All of my senses were aroused by his presence. I felt his warmth, his breathing, and a subtle exotic scent made my nostrils tingle. My whole being was enveloped by his presence!

'Your cue, Annabel!' Our stage manager, text in hand, pulled me out of my trance. He pushed me onto the stage and into my part. My scene over, I had to exit where Sebastian was still waiting for his entrance. While he stepped out of the wings, he touched my hand, ever so lightly – by accident? I felt my heart thumping in my chest, thumping so hard I could hardly breathe. I raced down the stairs to the dressing room.

'Slow down, Annabel.' Hanna, her part over, was removing her makeup. 'You are all out of breath.' She looked at me quizzically. 'Are you alright? You look . . . hot!'

'I'm fine,' I assured her in as normal a voice as I could manage, 'I'm perfect.'

But I wasn't. I was all shook up and confused. Oh, my good fairy, what was happening to me? He is just flirting, my fairy answered, that touch didn't mean anything . . . it meant nothing . . . nothing . . .

The next night we stood together in the dark again. Was he coming up early to catch me before my entrance?

'You are early,' I whispered.

'I like to watch your scene,' he whispered back – his warm breath brushing my ear.

The Snoop was hanging around back-stage, though she wasn't on till the next act. I didn't dare wait for Sebastian. I disappeared as soon as my scene was over – my mind in a dither, my body aching for his touch.

My confusion, my longing for him, kept me in a state of suspense. Not even Madame Cloutot's breathing exercises, practiced more ardently than ever, were able to bring some semblance of normality to my troubled mind. There was no *Beaver Coat* scheduled for three days – three days without a glimpse of Sebastian. He was, I knew, at rehearsal during the day. He had landed a dream part in a new play about the young Alexander. His was the title role, Alexander the Great, the Greek conqueror of continents, whom I had dreamed about in history class.

On the second day without Sebastian, I sneaked into the darkened theatre where he was rehearsing. I sat down in the last row. The Snoop was sitting in the front row beside the Beerbelly, who was directing. She was cast as Roxanne, the young Alexander's love object.

'Hello Annabel.' Hanna's whispered voice startled me. 'Thought I might find you here.' She sat down beside me. 'Isn't it pathetic that the Snoop was cast as 'a nymph-like creature' – at least that's what it says in the text. She looks like a Brunhilde beside Sebastian! She's much too tall and too solid. '*Na ja*,' she sighed, 'another miscast due to favouritism. You should be Roxanne, Annabel, but I didn't expect the Beerbelly to cast you as Sebastian's partner.'

'Why not! I didn't know he disliked me.'

'He's jealous – that's why! He is more devious than he makes you believe. I saw him watching the two of you at rehearsal – and when you were standing together in the wings – he must have noticed . . .'

'Noticed what?' I said too fast. 'What could he have noticed?'

'That there are certain vibrations between you two – at least that's what I noticed.'

I couldn't lie to Hanna. 'I didn't know it was that obvious . . .'

'It isn't Annabel – but I happen to know that the Beerbelly has a thing for Sebastian.'

'What? Are you telling me he is homosexual? No, not him! He takes his wife to every first-night party, and he adores his little daughter . . .'

'That has nothing to do with it! You are so naïve Annabel! There are all sorts of sexual attractions and arrangements. Look at our main character actor, celebrated Herr von Herrle! He's obviously intimate with our young heroine - yet he lives with his wife and daughter. Ménage à trois, it's called. It seems his wife has no trouble sharing him.'

'I could never share the man I love - never!'

Hanna gave me a sideways look.

'Never say never, Annabel – never.'

What a relief! The good fairy hadn't deserted me. A new and unexpected part demanded my full attention. Our mighty, unapproachable top boss had decided to revive a British comedy from last season, and take it to the spa towns. I had to fill the part of my oh-so-popular predecessor once again. My colleagues hastened to tell me how convincing she had been as the young working-class girl who inspires a tense bourgeois accountant to loosen up. Once again the pressure was on! This time the Beerbelly granted me five days of rehearsal. My confidence started to sprout like the grass in spring. The costume department sewed a tight dress for me, and the hairdresser swept my mane into a pony tail. I liked the way I looked – sexy. My lines, written by J.B. Priestley, were hilarious – the audience rewarded me with laughter. The prop man, when I entered the bus for our second performance, shouted: 'Annabel, I wasn't sure you had it in you, but you deliver what the blondes only promise.' Everybody laughed. Herr von Herrle, who had just come on board, took the empty seat beside me, and started a conversation. Had I finally been accepted? Was I fully out of the water? I felt like Mother Holle was raining her gold onto me after all.

My brief time of happiness came to an end at the next *Beaver Coat* performance. I was anxious to see Sebastian, to feel his presence in the dark, to be near him. Stop, don't be an idiot, I told myself. He hasn't searched you out for a whole week! Don't make a fool of yourself! I decided to come up for my scene at the last minute – no standing close to Sebastian in the dark.

'Annabel, you are on!' the stage manager came flying into our dressing room. 'What are you trying to do? Wreck your scene?' I'm trying not to wreck my life, I thought, as I scrambled up the stairs. I heard my cue as soon as I approached the stage. I had to go on – no chance to look for Sebastian, as planned. But he was there, in the dark of the wings, when I came off. Our eyes met.

'I missed you – I have a book I would like you to read . . . oh sorry, my cue . . .' He was gone.

Should I wait for him – did I dare? No, move girl – move! I couldn't – my feet were glued to the boards. He had missed me . . . he wanted to see me . . .

'Listen Annabel,' the Snoop startled me. She must have been hanging around backstage as usual, watching me – us?

'Have you seen Sebastian as Alexander?' she whispered. I shook my head. I had been afraid to watch him. I was scared of what it would do to me! Sebastian in a short Greek costume with shiny breastplate for two-and-a-half hours! And the Snoop as his sweetheart, being held and being kissed by him - too painful! I had decided to forgo this torture.

'Oh you must come and see us,' the Snoop blathered on. 'Sebastian is brilliant – and he looks gorgeous – there's always a bunch of teenagers waiting for him after the performance, begging for his autograph. Did you know?'

'I can imagine it . . .' I mumbled.

Sebastian, getting off the stage, joined us. The Snoop took his arm and we walked downstairs together. Sebastian's part was finished, I had a couple more scenes, and the Snoop was on to the end. Before Sebastian could disappear into his dressing room, the Snoop held him back by taking one of his hands.

'Please wait for me,' she cooed, 'I want to walk home with you . . . I don't like walking along this quiet street of mine in the dark.'

Well done, Snake! You know how to get what you want! I saw another Bruna, who had stolen my lover in Berlin, slithering out of the closet. The Snoop's tactics made me feel like a child – not old enough to play the game.

Chapter 25

Another rotten night! I had been either wide-awake or asleep having a nightmare. I dreamed Sebastian and I had a scene together – he was waiting for me on-stage – I'm not ready – I don't know what play it is - there's not a smidgen of makeup on my face – I try to put on some lipstick but my hand is shaking - there are red smudges all over my face - I reach for the hem of my skirt to wipe them off, but there is no skirt, I'm naked – somebody pushes me onto the stage – I stand there shivering - Sebastian is gone – I'm all alone on the stage – somebody laughs – others join in – roaring laughter is rising out of the auditorium – I want to run away but my feet are stuck to the boards – I scream! And wake myself up.

I felt drowsy. The bright light hurt my eyes. The church bell struck ten o'clock. Luckily there was no rehearsal. I stretched and looked out the window. A sunny spring day greeted me. Birds were chirping in the graveyard non-stop. I watched them fly back and forth with blades of dry grass in their beaks. They were building their nests. I had to get out into the spring air, forget my nightmare, and forget Sebastian. Enjoy the day and not think of the future.

I decided to explore a new area, a part of town I had never visited. I left the old and familiar behind and followed the road into the country. I walked swiftly while I wrote a letter to Werner in my head.

'Dearest Darling, please come to me as soon as you can. I need your presence. I'm in danger! I have fallen in love with another man – I have no idea if he loves me – I need you to sort out my tormented brain – and my body that's aching for him . . .' No, that wouldn't do! Honesty is a fine thing, but in this case entirely misplaced. I started again: Dearest Werner, when will you be able to come and visit? I need to see you . . .' or maybe not? The squealing of brakes interrupted my thoughts. Sebastian, sitting on his Vespa, had stopped beside me.

'Glad I caught you Annabel. Did you have to get out too – on a day like this? Jump on – let's get out of town.' Oh yes, yes, let's – my heart sang.

'Don't you have rehearsal today?' I said out loud.

'No, our head director travelled to Hamburg today, looking for new talent.' To replace me, flashed through my mind. Forget it! Don't let anything spoil your joy! I jumped on behind Sebastian, wrapped my arms around his waist, and off we went.

'Can you slow down please,' I screamed into his ear when he shifted into top gear. I was used to riding on my moped at thirty kilometres maximum, now I was zooming along, my hair flying, my dress ballooning around me, and my heart ready to jump out of my chest.

'You are perfectly safe,' Sebastian shouted back . . . just hold on tight!' There was nothing I liked better.

In minutes we were out of town, sailing along a country road. Soft hills, clusters of forest, sloping meadows bathed in sunshine, a few cows resting in the shade of a tree doing their endless chewing. I tightened my arms around Sebastian, felt his firm midriff, noticed the blond stubble on his tanned neck, and stifled an impulse to kiss him behind the ear.

'Relax, Annabel,' Sebastian shouted. Had he noticed the tightness in my arms? 'I won't open her up all the way!'

'I'm fine now,' I shouted in his ear, 'I trust you!' But I couldn't relax – my heart was thumping so fast.

After half an hour of this joyous, torturous closeness, Sebastian turned his head and shouted, 'Let's stop at the *Waldschenke*, I'm getting thirsty.'

We were the only customers. We chose a table outside in the *Biergarten*. The innkeeper, still in his work overalls, placed a couple of beers in front of us. Sebastian insisted on paying.

'I so enjoy talking to you Annabel.' Beer foam on his lips, Sebastian put down his glass. 'You are the only person in the ensemble who seems to be interested in things other than the theatre . . . and you keep to yourself! I like that.'

'You mentioned a book . . . what is it about?' I was glad I had thought of it.

'It's called *Siddhartha*, written by Hermann Hesse. I've told you about my interest in eastern religious practices, meditation in particular. Hesse's story is about a young man who sets out to find enlightenment, or as we would say, peace, the peace that passes all understanding.'

'That reminds me of a postcard I found in a bookstore depicting the face of Saint Anne. Her picture, I learned, was part of a famous painting by Leonardo da Vinci. Her facial expression spoke to me. She looked like she had found the peace you are talking about. I just had to buy the card.'

'It's a long and arduous way to complete peace; only a few saints have ever reached it. The yogis call it *samadhi*, the state of bliss. Hesse writes that first of all you have to experience life, the mundane life, then work on letting it go - which means you have to overcome your ego and drop all desire.' Why did he have to mention that last word? I was willing to overcome a lot of things – food, drink – but not my desire for him. I couldn't – it wasn't in my power.

'Yes, I can see how hard that is - not wanting anything. As actors we are always hoping that the next good part will be ours; we are hoping for a good critique, for the audience to applaud us and . . .'

'You are so right – sometimes I truly hate my profession. I hate the fact that it pleases me when teenagers ask for my autograph. I don't want to stoop to Karin's level. I'm sure she would offer herself to the Queen Bee, as you call him, for a leading role.'

'Haha, the Queen Bee! I don't think there's a flying chance he would take her up on the offer.'

We laughed. The sun, now high above us, made Sebastian's eyes take on the colour of the sky. I looked down fast – I mustn't let him see how much I wanted him. One of his hands was curled around his beer glass. I noticed his long, slim fingers, his sunburned hand, the golden hairs on it . . . Sebastian, oh Sebastian, what are you doing to me?

'Oh . . . good that you are back, Fräulein Lambert.' Peter, whom I suspected of keeping track of my movements, came running out of the house as soon as I had jumped off Sebastian's Vespa. 'Herr Helwig called. He's coming tomorrow . . . leaving early from Düsseldorf.' He gave Sebastian a long look. 'I told your fiancée you'll be glad to see him.'

Werner here tomorrow! I said goodbye to Sebastian and fled up to my room. I sat down on the bed. I stared at the church tower, so stark, so strong, and my mind all churned up, my body weak with desire. Only a few hours ago I had composed a letter to Werner – I need you, please come as soon as possible – now I was afraid to see him, to be with him! How would I be able to make love to him when I wanted Sebastian, when I needed to be with Sebastian, when every fibre in my body was longing for him?

That night, I tossed and turned in my bed once again. At midnight, the twelve deep bongs of the church bell made me shiver. The weather had turned. The wind made the shutters rattle. An angry rain knocked against the windowpanes. Was the big bad wolf going to get me? Had I strayed too far from the well-trodden path?

Chapter 26

I had expected Werner to be waiting in my room when I returned from rehearsal the next day. But he wasn't. Maybe he had changed his mind because of the weather? Had he called? I knocked on my landlady's door.

'No, no call,' she said. She turned down the radio. 'The poor boy, likely got stuck in the rain. I've been listening to the news . . . they warned about flooding on some of the country roads.'

I went back to my room and unpacked three bottles of beer and a half bottle of *Genever*. Werner deserved something special after his long ride – or did I want to relieve my guilty conscience when I purchased the intoxicants for him?

I lay down on the bed and worked on my lines for the next play, the last of the season, *The Potting Shed* by Graham Greene. My part, Anne, was a twelve-year-old girl! Was that an improvement over the twelve- year-old boy in *The Winter's*

Tale? How much longer did I have to play the super innocent? My mind drifted. What if Werner had an accident? What if he was lying in a hospital – dying? It would be my fault – I had betrayed him in my heart! I got up and opened a bottle of beer. It was getting dark outside, and the rain hadn't stopped. Where was he? I finished the beer and poured myself just a thimble full of *Genever*. Oh heavenly Saint Anne, let him be alright, let him be safe!

Clink . . . clink . . . I woke up. What was that? Clink . . . clink . . . that sound again. It came from my windows. I had closed them to keep the rain out. Clink . . . clink . . . there it was again! I dragged myself, half- asleep, to one of the windows and looked down. There, eerily illuminated by the only streetlight on my road, stood Werner, his moped by his side, his arm raised about to throw another stone. He looked wet and disheveled. He dropped the stone and smiled up at me. The house was dark and quiet. What time was it? I tiptoed down the stairs and opened the front door.

'You poor, poor man,' I whispered. 'What happened? Are you alright?'

'I'm wonderful,' he whispered back, 'now that I'm holding you in my arms.'

I was so glad he wasn't hurt, I hugged him back and kissed him. Upstairs I helped him out of his wet clothes while he told me how his moped had quit on him in the rain, and how a friendly man at a gas station had managed to start it up again, and he hadn't even charged him for it. We crawled onto the bed and puffed up the pillows behind our backs. I poured us each a glass of beer and a shot of *Genever.*

'Strictly medicinal,' I said, 'I don't want you to catch a cold.'

We fell into the familiar pattern – drinking, talking, laughing.

Werner mimicked his director, a bald little man, who blew up at everybody and everything except his mistress, a proper countess – and a poor actress. He cast her in all major roles, or better, only put on plays in which he could display her! Typical! After a while Werner flattened his pillow, pulled me under the covers, and made love to me. It was fine. He fell asleep with his arms wrapped tightly around me. I listened to his regular breathing. Then, as usual, I untangled myself, rolled onto my other side, and fell asleep.

I had three comfortable days with him. On one of those days we went for a ride in the country on our mopeds. Not in the direction of the *Waldschenke,* I had told him. Let's drive to Bad Meetberg and take the waters. Bad Meetberg we went – but we opted for beer. We saved the healing waters for the arthritic pensioners who hobbled along the paths of the spa gardens.

On day four I had a rehearsal. I was hoping I wouldn't meet Sebastian – I didn't want to be all stirred up again. No such luck!

'Enjoying yourself,' Sebastian greeted me, 'you look well contented.'

The Snoop! She couldn't keep her blabbermouth shut. Werner and I had met her in town. She must have spurted away to inform the entire ensemble that Annabel's boyfriend was visiting again. Sheer jealousy – she didn't have a man of her own. Sex, I wasn't sure about. She was on hugging and kissing terms with several of the male actors.

'When is Werner leaving?' Sebastian asked. He must have noticed I wasn't going to comment on my contentment.

'Tomorrow . . . he has rehearsal the day after.' Why did I feel the need to explain his departure? Did I want Sebastian to know Werner was devoted to me, that he would stay forever if he could?

'Good.' Sebastian walked towards the Beerbelly who was directing. Halfway he turned around and smiled. 'Good,' he repeated.

I had promised myself I was going to be as calm as a lake when there's no wind - his presence wouldn't be able to stir up the slightest ripple. But as I walked out the stage door my heart was a-flutter. Good, he had said. What was good? That Werner was leaving? That I looked contented? You're no good Sebastian, no good at all! You trouble me - you're stirring up a longing in me I cannot control! Oh Saint Anne of eternal peace, help me! Don't let the big bad wolf catch me.

First night of *The Potting Shed.* I was nervous. The all-powerful top boss was in the audience – and my contract hadn't been renewed yet. How convincing can a twenty-four-year old woman portray a twelve-year-old girl on stage? Would flattening my breasts and putting me into a child's dress do the trick this time? My faithful friend Hanna said I looked convincing – from a distance. And she was right. The audience didn't boo at me. They clapped when I took my bow.

I was glad to run into one of the older actors when I left the theatre. He offered to accompany me to the pub for our first-night celebration. I hadn't planned on going – there were too many things on my mind: Why had my contract not been renewed? Was I the only one who hadn't heard from the mighty all-powerful man upstairs? Would Sebastian show up? Did I want him to?

Now, in the company of my old colleague, I changed my mind. He was a kind man, not obsessively ambitious. I had played his daughter in a comedy, and he hadn't resented the laughs I got, though he was the main comedian in the play. He took me by the hand, like my poor Papa used to do, and told me about his loneliness – his wife and children lived so far away he only got to see them during our long summer break. 'My wife is getting fed up with the situation. Last summer she suggested I look for another job. I told her it was too late for that. Don't marry an actor, Annabel, there is so much separation – and so much temptation.' He squeezed my hand. 'In the beginning it was exciting. We enjoyed a honeymoon every time we got together – not now. Now I would like to come home to my own place, not the rented room I inhabit here, put up my feet and have my woman look after me. Instead I have to converse intelligently with our oh-so-artistic director. If he gets into Samuel Beckett and Nihilism again, I'm going to throw up. Theatre should be above all entertainment – life is bleak enough. It makes me feel warm inside if I make people laugh – make them forget their problems for a couple of hours.' We had reached our destination. 'Let's sit well away from the intelectuals,' he whispered as we entered the pub. 'I'm grateful for the company of a young, honest actress like you, Annabel - and for a cold beer.'

My eyes scanned the crowd – no Sebastian. Why hadn't he joined the cast? The Snoop had, though she wasn't in the play. She had managed to squeeze in between the Queen Bee and the Beerbelly. I watched her. She laughed out loud at their jokes, she 'accidentally' touched their arms, and at one point she got up and started to knead the Queen Bee's shoulders! He had mentioned how worn out he felt. Her schmoozing was in high gear. Hanna, who was sitting beside me, had been observing the Snoop's performance as well.

'Look at her, Annabel, watch her,' she whispered. 'If you want your contract to be renewed you better start to act – behind the stage – right here.'

'Flirt with the Queen?' I whispered back. 'He'd think I'm a total ignoramus, too naïve to know his sexual orientation.'

'You're hopeless, Annabel, look at the Snoop – there's not a man on earth who doesn't like to be adored – no matter what his sexual orientation is.'

Chapter 27

No more rehearsals in the morning meant lots of time on my hands – oh how I hated that! Right now I needed a distraction more than ever before. In a month the theatre season would be over. When, at Werner's last visit, I had shared my worries about not having been offered a new contract, he had suggested that I forget the *Landestheater* and move into a flat with him in Düsseldorf.

'There are two subsidized theatres in the city, and two private companies. We are bound to find employment.'

'You would, I'm sure. There are so many more men needed than women. Look at all the classical plays. Men, men, men – and two or three women. I can't see myself sitting at home waiting for the phone to ring. I would go mad!'

'But you wouldn't be lonely . . . we would be together every night! We would go to places together when we are free. Düsseldorf has been completely rebuilt. The Königsallee is a fashionable avenue with beautiful shops and cafés . . . and there is a huge park, ten times the size of the Duke's estate here . . . and a lake with all sorts of ducks and swans. You would like it, I tell you.'

I knew I was in no shape to make a rational decision about my future. How could I? My brain, my heart and all of my senses were taken over by that alluring being named Sebastian . . . Sebastian.

'I have to think about it, Werner – give me some time . . . maybe . . .' I had left the word hanging in the air. Maybe – it was a word of hope, wasn't it?

We had performed the Priestley play in Bad Salzach. Sebastian, who had a minor part, hadn't spoken to me since his mysterious 'good' statement. I was aching to talk to him, to touch him, but I didn't dare. After the show, I took my regular seat on the bus without so much as looking for him. To my surprise, Sebastian, who always sat in front beside the Beerbelly, plunked himself down next to me. My heart was singing, my mind doing somersaults.

'I've read more of *Siddhartha,*' he said. 'I'm sure Hesse not only studied eastern religions and practices, but got actively involved. I'm not sure yet if he ever went to India – I'll have to find out. Everything he writes makes so much sense – and is so different from our western, autocratic religions.'

He had placed his beautiful hands on his knees – so close to mine. Oh did I want to touch them! 'I guess that's why I don't go to church anymore,' I said instead. 'Our father who art in heaven . . . we now know that there isn't anything like heaven, just space and planets and stars.'

'I like the Brahmins concept of God. He's neither the benevolent father nor the punishing judge. He is the ultimate truth, beyond human understanding . . . and he's inherent in every living thing . . . so non-violence becomes a logical necessity.'

I was captured by his hand – so close to mine – what had he said? Was he waiting for a comment? Something about non-violence . . .

'You mean the way Mahatma Gandhi lived and taught,' I was glad his name had come to my rescue. I wanted Sebastian to know I shared his interest, and I did! It was just so darn hard to concentrate when he was so close – my mind went blank in his presence – my desire took over my brain.

'Yes, exactly. He was one of those rare people who lived what he taught. No wonder he was murdered – like Christ. We humans don't seem to be able to accept absolute goodness – it frightens us . . . oh, by the way,' Sebastian put his hand on mine and an electric current ran up and down my spine, 'we are having a reading at my place tomorrow. Our director suggested it when I mentioned my fascination with *Siddhartha*. Good old Helene offered to read Rilke, and our stage manager is eager to take part as well. And Karin, naturally, I couldn't keep her away! She told me, in confidence, she'll do Margaret's prayer in the cathedral. I had to smile when she said it. She knows Goethe's *Faust* is on the program for next season. She wants to make sure she'll be cast as Margaret.'

Margaret, how I had laboured with that part at school – and how finally I had made it mine with the scene in the dungeon when she struggles with a mind that has escaped reality. How I had wallowed in the ever-changing torment of her emotions! The old geezer, disinterested in anything I delivered, had muttered some comments for the first time. Forget it, Annabel, the Snoop will get the part. You don't have a hope in Mephistopheles' hell!

'So will you come . . . I would like you to be there.' Sebastian's hand had slid onto mine again and brought me back with an electric shock.

'Sure,' I managed to say, 'what time?'

There was no performance that day, so the meeting was set for eight. He gave me his address.

As I climbed the stairs to Sebastian's third floor home, my feelings were a jumble. Delight, confusion, insecurity were having a wrestling match. Why had he invited me? He hadn't asked me to contribute. Was I the only listener while everybody else performed?

The room, right under the roof like mine, with slanted walls on two sides, resounded with voices and laughter when I entered. The Snoop was sitting next to the Beerbelly on the couch, old Helene was sprawled out on the floor oohing and aahing while our stage manager was rubbing her feet. One of the young actors the Snoop hung around with was pouring wine into water glasses. I spotted an empty place and, crossing my legs, let myself down onto the floor. I took the glass I was offered, happy not to receive further attention.

Sebastian was the first to read. I allowed his beautiful voice to calm me. I closed my eyes and imagined he was reading only for me. When he stopped, I had to open my eyes again - but I didn't dare look at him. The Beerbelly commented on the text, and the Snoop made a few smart remarks so everybody understood how 'intelligent' she was. Then she went into Margaret's cathedral scene. I hated to admit it – her performance was touching. Maybe her voice sounded too adult in places, too sure . . . still, she knew her craft. Obviously she had worked on it. The Snoop left nothing to chance! Helene, who had played my mother in a couple of shows, now read Rilke from a thin volume called *A Poem of Love and Death*. I had never heard of it, and the language, so brief, so poetic, grabbed me deep inside and released a flood of emotions. I couldn't help tears flooding my eyes when the actress read ' . . . *what one man is talking about, they all have experienced, just like him – as if there was only ONE mother . . .*' MOTHER, not stepmother – I didn't even know mine! To squeeze the tears out before anybody could notice, I shut my eyes tightly. When I opened them, I saw Sebastian looking at me. His glance was serious and sad in a way. I felt so close to him! Oh how I wanted to hug him – to be hugged by him!

The official part over, the Beerbelly produced another bottle of wine, and I managed to exchange a few sentences with the stage manager. He wasn't without ambition, I learned. He had been cast in a few walk-on parts when nobody else was available, and he had caught the bug. He was hoping to get into some serious acting. As he belonged to the Queen Bee's hive, I was sure he had a chance.

The party broke up around midnight. Suddenly, while I was putting on my jacket in the hall, Sebastian was at my side. 'Wait, Annabel,' he whispered, and out loud, 'Annabel hang on please . . . I'll find the book you wanted to borrow . . . I'll be right back!' He led the gang down the stairs. He had to lock the big front door behind them. I stood alone in the room. My heart was pounding. What book? I hadn't asked him for a book? I heard Sebastian jump up the stairs, two steps at a time. He entered, breathing hard. We looked into each other's eyes, for how long? Then Sebastian stepped forward and took me in his arms. He kissed me. 'Don't be afraid,' he murmured. Had I been holding back? I closed my eyes and allowed my lips to open.

Ring . . . ring . . . riiiiing! The bell cut us apart. 'Damn,' Sebastian muttered, 'who can that be?' Riiiiing . . . long. Someone was holding his finger on the bell. 'Damn,' Sebastian muttered again, 'I can't pretend I've gone to bed – the lights are on . . .' He flew down the stairs – came up with the Beerbelly.

'I forgot my spectacles, Annabel,' our director explained. He started to look around the room. We all looked – no glasses. 'But I used them here, remember? When I read . . .' his voice trailed off. He hadn't read anything. The three of us kept searching. No spectacles showed up.

'Sorry, Sebastian, I must have dropped them in the car . . .' The Beerbelly, not in the least concerned, turned towards the door. 'Oh Annabel,' he took a couple of steps back, 'I'll give you a ride home – you wouldn't want to be out in the dark alone at this hour?' Sebastian and I exchanged glances behind his back.

'Thank you, that's very kind of you,' I managed to mumble.

'It's a pleasure, Annabel. I know you are not afraid to walk at night, but I feel better if you don't – and Sebastian here needs his beauty sleep – *The Young Alexander* is on tomorrow.'

On the short drive to my room, the Beerbelly chatted about Sebastian's extraordinary talent, and how easily it could be squandered if he didn't stay focussed. 'Once you have felt success, it's hard to keep working, to keep up the desire to reach greater heights,' he said. 'Sebastian is committed, no doubt, but there is always the danger of distraction – you know what I mean . . .' he patted my hand. We had reached my house. 'Thanks for the drive,' I said. I climbed out of the car and banged the door shut! – And thanks for the lecture, you two-faced old trickster, I muttered to myself.

Though it was late, sleep was no comfort. I still felt his kiss on my lips. I tried to remember every look, every touch we had shared. Had it really happened? Did he want me? Oh, my good fairy . . . oh Saint Anne of eternal peace . . . let it be true . . . please let it be true!

Chapter 28

The sun had already come around the house when I awoke. It flooded my room with brightness. Last night's event, as bright as the sunlight, flooded my mind. He wanted me! It was no accident, his kiss! He had carefully planned for us to be together – alone. Oh wonderful, wonderful day!

I jumped out of bed and danced down to the bathroom. I splashed cold water on my face and brushed my teeth, long, thoroughly. I washed with care. Breathe out – feel your tummy descend – let the tension flow out with the breath. Madame Cloutot's words were ringing in my ears. Breathe out – let the tension flow out . . . out . . . out . . . It worked. I felt calmer. Good eccentric Madame, good old sorceress!

I dressed – my favourite blouse and a new skirt, purchased under protest from my budget. I brushed my hair up into a ponytail, and tied a ribbon around it. I took my hand mirror and studied my profile. I liked what I saw.

There was no way I could concentrate on anything other than Sebastian. Cleaning my room, reading, writing a letter to my Papa or to my brother – things I would normally occupy myself with, were out of the question. I had to get out of my room – get out and walk. After circling the pond in the castle estate three times, I stopped. A few water lilies had opened up and were spreading their whiteness onto the flat green leaves. I focussed my eyes on the reflection of the sun on the water – motion in liquid gold – a different pattern with the slightest change of breeze . . .

'Hello Annabel, I see the sun lured you outside as well.' Hanna appeared at my side. 'Did you notice the swans – how closely they stick together? They mate for life, did you know?' When I didn't answer, Hanna took my hand. 'Be careful Annabel, and . . .' she looked straight into my eyes, 'think before you jump, promise?' I nodded. I didn't want Hanna to go into details – I didn't want to talk about something even she wouldn't understand, nobody would.

Suddenly I felt an urge to go home to my room – I said, adieu, so long, to my friend, and rushed off. In my room, I cleared a couple of books and a letter from Werner off the table. I smoothed out the blanket on my bed. I looked at my alarm clock – not yet two. A knock on my door startled me. I pushed a strand of hair behind my ear, bit on my lip, and opened the door.

Sebastian, it was him!

For a second we just stood there.

'Come in . . .' I finally managed to stutter.

'The house door was open,' he said. 'I didn't mean to intrude on you.'

'Oh it's alright, I wasn't doing anything, it's no intrusion.' The words came tumbling out of my mouth.

'I thought I better bring you that book I promised you last night.' I saw the flicker in his eyes. We laughed. He placed the volume he was holding in his hand on the table. When I tried to pick it up, he caught my hand and pulled me towards him. 'It's not about the book, Annabel, you know that. It's about us.' My heart, already beating in my throat, was about to jump right out of it.

Sebastian led me to my bed, sat me down, took me into his arms and kissed me – gentle, sweet, probing kisses. My eyes had closed – and my brain. My body, my senses were all I was. His kisses became more demanding, more passionate. Every fibre of my body responded. Like a flower stretching for the light it reached for him, wanted to get closer to him, wanted to merge with him! I felt Sebastian open, slowly, the buttons of my blouse, then the clasp of my bra. He drew back and gazed at me. 'You have beautiful breasts, Annabel, just the right size. They fit my hands perfectly.' He cupped his hands around them and kissed my nipples, first one, then the other. I felt myself taken over by a force that wasn't mine to guide or change. As you can't prevent a waterfall from tumbling down, so I couldn't stop giving myself to him. Oh Sebastian, Sebastian, my heart was singing while my body felt sensations new and surprising.

He wasn't finished in a few seconds after we had come together – no, he asked me to tell him when I wanted him to come – when *I* would want him to come! I was so swept away I forgot to mumble my fear of pregnancy. He took care without being asked.

Quiet now, we lay in each other's arms. Sebastian didn't fall asleep, he talked.

'Are you alright, Annabel . . . did it feel right?'

'Oh ja, ja,' I whispered. I buried my face in his shoulder so he wouldn't notice the tears in my eyes – my tears of joy.

'I don't know . . . I felt you were holding back . . . not intentionally, I'm sure . . . just unable to surrender . . .'

It was all new and so different for me, I wanted to answer, but didn't.

'Be my teacher,' I said instead, 'you'll be surprised how fast I'll learn.' Was that *me* talking? Where did that boldness come from?

'I would like to give you another lesson right now,' Sebastian gave me a brief kiss. He was leaning on his elbow, his hair all ruffled up, a warm glow on his cheeks. He looked like a beautiful, aristocratic boy, the kind you'd find in a Gainsborough painting. 'Unfortunately I have to leave. I always do a bit of voice training, and go over certain scenes, before *Alexander.* That part takes a lot of energy! Did you notice, I'm in every single scene but one?' I hadn't, because I had been too afraid to watch him with the Snoop as his love object. Now that I knew he wanted *me*, I was looking forward to seeing him in his star role. I kissed him and smiled.

Himmelhoch jauchzend – zu Tode betrübt, shouting with joy – grieved to death, these famous words of Goethe described my state of being to perfection. He liked me . . . he wanted me . . . he loved me? Had I disappointed him when we made love? I thought of Daniel, my first love, at the school in Berlin. Sebastian was a lot like him, only more sure of himself, more mature. Bruna had kept a hold on Daniel - because of her sexual expertise? I had wondered about that. I loved Sebastian - I wanted him! Why had I not been able to fully surrender, as he had called it? Would he want to try again – would he want to make love to me again? Shouting with joy – grieved to death! Good old Goethe, you knew the human heart! You must have experienced the state I was in! I grabbed one of the volumes of Goethe's collected works, a Christmas present from my brother, and began to read *The Suffering of the Young Werther.* I had started on the story once before without finishing it. Now, as I read, I became absorbed in his language, and the words he used to express his feelings! I was captured by Goethe's insight and his honesty.

I was living for the moment when I would see Sebastian again – on *Beaver Coat* night, only one night and one day away - though it felt like weeks. But finally, there we were again, standing in the wings, in the dark, waiting for our cues. He took my hand

and squeezed it – then moved away fast. The Snoop had come up. As usual, she wasn't going to miss Sebastian. She didn't pay any attention to me, but whispered something in his ear. You bitch, I wanted to scream, he's never going to sleep with you! You can offer yourself as much as you want! He likes *me* – he wants *me*! Oh, my bad fairy! Do your *Sleeping Beauty* trick! Please, prick her finger and send her into a century-long sleep!

In the few seconds between my exit and Sebastian's entry, he looked around . . . then whispered, 'Come to my place after the performance. I'll make sure the house door is open . . . don't ring the bell.'

I skipped down the stairs to our dressing room. I blew out my breath a few times before I entered. Calm, calm – nobody must sense my happiness.

Chapter 29

I said good night to Hanna and another actor who happened to walk out the stage door with me, and started off in the direction of my room. When my colleagues were out of sight, I turned into a narrow alley and made my way over to Sebastian's house. Yes, the door was unlocked! It creaked when I opened it. I climbed up the stairs placing my feet down gently, gently, and made it up the three flights evoking only two creaks. Sebastian's door was ajar, and I slipped in, quiet as a cat. My love closed the door and locked it.

The table was set: candles, wine glasses, and open face sandwiches, artfully arranged. He took my jacket, dropped it on a chair, and pulled me close. He smiled at me – I saw a warm glow in his eyes. I felt like Anna Karenina who had stolen herself away from her husband, and had come to be with her beloved cavalry officer.

'I thought you must be hungry,' Sebastian pulled me down onto the couch beside him. 'You told me you are used to eating after the performance – and so am I.' He poured the wine and to my surprise, I had an appetite. I enjoyed the sandwiches. I was hungry.

'I'd like to read a short passage from *Siddhartha* to you,' he said after he had cleared the table. 'It made a profound impression on me, it made me think . . .' He took the small volume and opened it where he had inserted a slip of paper. 'Siddhartha has met the beautiful courtesan Kamala,' he explained, 'he has asked her to be his teacher in love and sex. Listen:

> He learned many things from her wise red lips. Her smooth gentle hand taught him many things. He, who was still a boy as regards love and was inclined to plunge to the depth of it blindly and insatiably, was taught by her that one cannot have pleasure without giving it, and that every gesture, every caress, every touch, every glance, every single part of the body has its secret which can give pleasure to one who can understand.'

Sebastian took my hand, raised it to his face, and held it to his cheek. He kept holding my hand in his as he read on.

> 'She taught him that lovers should not separate from each other after making love without admiring each other, without being conquered as well as conquering, so that no feeling of satiation or desolation arises nor the horrid feeling of misusing or having been misused.'

He closed the book, took both of my hands into his, and looked into my eyes. 'How do you feel about that, Annabel . . . do you agree?'

I love you, I love you, I love you is all I could think, is all I wanted to say! 'Oh ja, it's beautiful,' I said out loud. For a moment I was afraid he didn't want to make love to me, because he felt he was using me to satisfy his own desire. 'And . . . and Hesse is right, the feeling has to be mutual. I can't imagine ever making love to a man I had no deep feelings for . . . sex without love . . . how can anybody . . . it's beyond me.'

'But how do you feel about making love to me – a married man?' There was concern in Sebastian's voice – did he feel guilty?

'I would be very disappointed if you didn't. I don't feel guilty, I . . .'

And it was true. I felt drawn to him like he was a magnet whose pull I had no power to resist. 'I feel that what we have has nothing to do with anybody else,' I said. I was overwhelmed by the force of my desire for him! I couldn't imagine that any harm might be caused by it. I accepted our love like the good fairy had bestowed it on us. A gift, a present. How could we waste it?

In bed together, Sebastian took his time. He stroked me, he kissed me, and he talked. He made sure I liked and enjoyed every kiss, every touch. When he was holding me in his arms afterwards, he brushed a few strands of hair out of my face. 'How do you feel,' he said, 'I wonder – you are so different, Annabel – but lovely. With you I feel like I'm making love to a virgin – your face is so full of surprise and excitement when we are together . . .' We kissed, we talked, we stroked each other, and then we made love again. Sebastian was able to do that – I noticed with joy. Later, we got dressed and slunk away on velvet paws like two children, who had just raided a well-stocked larder. The streets were quiet – not a single car passed us. A dog started to bark behind a fence. Two BOOMS struck from the steeple of the church when Sebastian kissed me good night at my door.

I didn't have to wait for sleep to start dreaming. I was in a dream, the most glorious, most exciting, most lovely dream I had ever dreamed. My prince had come, and he had taken me on his white horse, and no witch, no bad wolf could ever spoil this dream in my heart.

Neither of us could hide our embarrassment, though my brother and his wife were tactful. They pretended not to notice that they had surprised Sebastian and me in bed. Anyway, they could have let me know they were dropping in for a visit!

'Oh, glad to meet you,' Hans exclaimed and shook Sebastian's hand. 'I've heard you are a great success as Alexander.' My love brushed back his hair in an unsuccessful attempt to straighten it out. I noticed his fly was only halfway up, and his shirttail was peeking out of the back of his trousers. I hadn't been able to close all the buttons on my blouse. I lifted the collar and fanned myself. 'Isn't it ever hot today,' I muttered. 'Don't you feel it's stifling here under the roof?'

Sebastian grabbed a book off my table. 'Thanks for letting me have this, Annabel,' he mumbled. 'I'll leave you to your company.' He said a quick goodbye and hurried out of my room.

'What a handsome man,' Christa's voice sounded softer than usual.

'Yes, indeed,' my brother added, 'more handsome than Werner, wouldn't you say, Anna?'

'I'm sorry but I didn't expect you. Shall I make some coffee?' I was determined to play it cool – as if nothing unusual had happened. I sent a prayer of thanks to my landlady. She had locked the front door when she went out – something she didn't always do when I was in the house.

Otherwise . . . I didn't even want to give it a thought.

Christa must have felt a sisterly alliance. She let the whole incident pass. She was eager to tell me her news.

'We are going to have another baby . . . I'm pregnant . . . finally. The doctor has confirmed it. There'll be a new family member.'

'Oh, how wonderful! I know how much you wanted this to happen!' I managed to congratulate her with a smiling face. Poor Hans! His son had been quite enough for him. Now she had managed to nail him down for good. Poor Hans! He looked worried. There were dark rings under his eyes. His forehead was furrowed with fine wrinkles. He had gained weight. His athletic figure was gone. Poor Hans! Youth had been driven out of him by family responsibilities – and by a boring, nagging, unimaginative wife.

I wasn't in the mood to chat with them. I couldn't stand how Christa always interrupted my brother, often contradicted him. I wanted to relive my lovemaking with Sebastian; I wanted to cuddle up in bed and dream about him.

'I'm sorry, but I need to be in the theatre early tonight. Our director wants to go over one of the scenes,' I lied. My brother got the hint and took charge of his wife for a change. I accompanied them to their car. When Christa was seated, he closed her door. Before he opened the driver's door he pulled me close and looked me straight in the eye. 'He's married, isn't he? Oh Anna, I hope you know what you are doing – I hope you know.'

Chapter 30

In three weeks the season would be over, and I still had no news about my contract. It worried me, but no more than an itch in the back of my neck. My non-stop ever-present worry was Sebastian. He was my last thought at night, before a restless sleep, and my first thought when I awoke. Would I get to see him? Would he come to my room again in the afternoon? I started to hang around the theatre in the morning hoping to meet him by chance. I turned into the Snoop and hated myself for it. Did I dare go to his flat, at night, after his show? What if the Beerbelly was with him – or if his wife had suddenly come back? I wasn't brave enough to take that chance. *The Beaver Coat* was the only show we shared, where I was sure to meet him. I couldn't wait that long! Please, wave your wand, my good fairy, and make him appear somehow, somewhere!

For three days I was Cinderella in her kitchen sitting not beside, but right on top of the hot cinders. On the fourth day

I found myself in the dark of night in a back alley, looking up to the light in his window. He was there, behind those walls, my love, my desire! I kept standing on the spot, looking up, sending a prayer to the good fairy to *please* make my prince appear.

'Meow, meow . . .' A cat had jumped off the roof of a shed next to me. It rubbed itself against my legs – it curled its body around and around them. I bent down and stroked it. It started to purr. I lifted it up and held it in my arms. It purred louder and rubbed his head against my chest. Suddenly a door opened. A stream of light hit the alley. I stepped back into the shade. 'Kiiiiitty . . . kitty, kitty, kitty . . .' The cat jumped out of my arms and disappeared into the next yard. Some grumbling, and the door was shut. When I looked up at Sebastian's window, it was dark. I slunk back to my room and cried myself to sleep.

A letter from Werner interrupted my non-stop thoughts of Sebastian. He would come to see me in a week's time! 'I have some exciting news, I'll tell you all about it when I'm with you,' he wrote. I sat at the table, staring at his handwriting. A knock on my door made my heart jump! I brushed back my hair, glanced into the mirror, and opened the door.

'There's a call for you, Fräulein Lambert.' Peter, smiling, peered past me into my room. Assured that I was alone, he delivered his message.

'My mother said to come down fast . . . it isn't Herr Werner,' he added.

It was the secretary of the great, all-powerful boss. I was to come to the office the next morning, ten o'clock sharp. To be sacked? Not likely. He would do that in writing. A new contract then – what else could it be?

'Sit down, Fräulein Lambert.' The great man greeted me without getting up from behind his huge desk. 'You must be wondering why you haven't been informed about your contract for the new season?' He lowered his spectacles and peered at me.

'Ja, I wasn't sure . . .' I mumbled. My heart was hammering against my chest with such force, I was afraid he might hear it.

'You had good reason to be unsure,' he interrupted my mumbling. 'I wasn't sure about your contract either – that's the reason for the delay. My head director has his doubts about you. He says you have a lisp. I didn't detect it when I saw you last in *The Potting Shed* . . . that was just a small part . . . but I have to trust his judgment . . . he has worked with you on several occasions.'

I was stunned. I had no words. My throat was as dry as the desert. I heard the grandfather clock behind me go tick-tock . . . tick-tock . . . Was he expecting an answer?

'Did you know about the lisp?' he asked after what seemed an endless pause. 'Weren't you told at Max-Reinhardt-Schule in Berlin, a school with a first-class reputation?'

'Nooo . . . I'll work on it . . . I'm sure I can . . .'

'You'll have to promise me that.' He looked over his glasses deep into my eyes, pushed the glasses up and focussed on a piece of paper in front of him.

'I have your contract here. Under the circumstances I'll not be able to give you an increase in salary, but . . . if I hear an improvement in your speech, and my two directors are happy with you, we can discuss money matters at a later date.' He pulled a fountain pen out of his breast pocket and handed it to me. 'You sign here, Fräulein Lambert.'

I signed.

My knees were shaking when I walked out of the office and shut the heavy wooden door behind me. A lisp . . . I had a lisp? Any defect in the speech of an actor is comparable to the dilemma a concert pianist has to face when he breaks a finger. How was it possible nobody had noticed such a calamity before? Was the Beerbelly behind the accusation? Be careful, Hanna had said, he is much more devious than he makes you believe. But he couldn't know about Sebastian and me . . . nobody did! We had been so careful!

I walked home in a daze. A lisp! I went through the s-exercises we had practiced in school. Soft sand sifting slowly . . . Was there a lisp?

I couldn't hear one.

At home, I walked back and forth in my room – I couldn't sit down. I read the new contract – nothing about a lisp, just the standard phrases. Still, I felt like I was rehired on approval – on the condition that my mysterious lisp would be gone.

How to face my colleagues? I was sure the Snoop already knew about it. She was in with the almighty ruler of the enterprise as well. She had been invited to his house once, she had bragged to me. And if the Snoop knew, everybody in the ensemble knew by now. I couldn't stand being alone any longer. I ran out of the house and to the nearest phone booth. My heart was pounding . . . but I had to talk to him . . . I had to share my anxiety . . . I had to hear the compassion in his voice . . . I had to see Sebastian! I knew he had his own telephone – would his number be in the book? I turned the pages with shaking fingers. Relief – he was in the book. I stared at the numbers. What if someone else answered? What if he said I can't see you? I steadied my breathing and dialed.

He agreed to meet me, as if by accident, in the castle gardens. My room didn't seem safe any more. When I saw him walking towards me I wondered – should I burden him with my worries? Hadn't he chosen to be with me because I shared his interests . . . I listened to his ideas . . . and he enjoyed making love to me?

'I'm glad you called me, Annabel Liebling, I care about your worries.' Sebastian's face showed sincere concern.

'Oh I'm so glad you don't mind. I wasn't sure if I should trouble you. You see, I haven't a single soul I can turn to here.'

'I'm glad you have come to me,' Sebastian repeated, 'but I think the Beerbelly has spied on us. We need to be more watchful.'

Sebastian must have noticed the sadness in my eyes. 'Oh, to hell with them! Come over after dark. Our spy is in a meeting tonight, and Karin has gone to visit a friend in B. I'll leave the front door open again.' He looked around, took my hand and gave it a fast squeeze. I had to draw on all the restraint inherent in me not to wrap my arms around his neck and cry on his shoulder.

Come, civil night, thou sober-suited matron, all in black . . . Juliet's words, spoken in anticipation of Romeo's visit to her bed, bubbled up in my mind. I wanted night to fall in a hurry so I could sneak to my lover's house, to be held in his arms, to be loved by him. My urgency was the same as hers, though heaven took its time to darken that day. Finally, at ten o'clock, I felt safe to start out for Sebastian's house. I didn't choose the most direct route. I made several detours through back alleys. When I turned into his street, I saw my comedy father walking towards me. Should I turn, run away? No – act casual – be calm! He waved to me as he came closer. I waved back.

'Hello Annabel,' he shouted when he reached me. 'Glad to meet you.' He put an arm around my shoulders. 'It's the funniest thing, you know. When I have five, six performances in a row, I complain, but now, when I'm free, I don't know what to do with myself.' I told him I felt the same way.

'Why don't you join me,' he said. 'I'll buy you a beer – come on!'

'I'm sorry, but I'm on my way to . . . Hanna. She's invited me for a goodbye party. You know she's leaving the theatre. It'll just be the two of us,' I added. I could rely on Hanna to cover my lie.

'Hm . . . enjoy yourself then, my girl.' My colleague sounded disappointed – or did he know something?

'I hope I don't have to face our super-artistic director and his entourage at the pub. I prefer to talk to the locals.'

I was glad he didn't detain me any longer, but went on his way. I walked past Sebastian's house in the direction of Hanna's. Soon as my colleague was out of sight, I turned. I looked around, then slipped into my lover's house. I climbed up the stairs slowly. I put my feet down close to the wall. I made it all the way up without a single creak.

Sebastian was on the telephone when I entered his room. I stepped back into the hall. His voice sounded agitated. I heard him say Helga. He was talking to his wife. When I heard him drop the receiver, I went back in. He was sitting on the couch, staring at the carpet in front of him.

'Bad news,' I asked, 'something happened?'

'Nothing I didn't expect . . . only I had hoped it wouldn't be so soon. Helga is coming home. She'll leave Düsseldorf around noon tomorrow – should arrive here by evening.'

My heart sank.

'Shall I leave . . . do you want me to go?'

Sebastian got up and walked towards me. He took my face into his hands.

'No, no – I'm glad you are here,' he kissed my eyes. 'Don't look so sad, Annabel. Remember . . . you said once what we have has nothing to do with anybody else . . . I had my doubts at the time . . . tonight I'm going to believe it.'

He turned off the lights and guided me into the bedroom.

'We'll keep all the lights off, then it'll look like I'm out. Oh, I forgot to lock the door downstairs.' He rushed out of the room. Back again, he lit a candle on the nightstand and shaded it with an open book. It was the title I had started to read: *The Suffering of the Young Werther* by Goethe.

'Are you reading this?'

'Yes, I recently dug it out again . . . it must be my third time.'

'I got back to it as well – and this time I can hardly put it down.'

We looked at each other. 'I feel so close to you . . . so close.' Sebastian's voice was full of tenderness.

We undressed, slipped under the comforter and talked. I told him about my Papa, how I had adored him, how he had made me feel safe, and how his new marriage had ruined our relationship . . . how I had promised to make his name known as the father of a famous actress . . . how I had let him down . . . how I wasn't able to bring any joy to his life.

Sebastian stroked my head and pulled his fingers through my hair.

'There are many more theatres in Germany, Annabel. Don't let two devious directors dampen your spirit. You know, I don't feel secure here either. Our almighty boss has hired a young man who will likely compete for my parts – and I'm sure with support from 'on high' will get them. He's tall, I'm told – the right size for a young hero - my one shortcoming,' he laughed.

I listened. How selfish I had been! Only concerned about my own grief. I lifted his hand off my breast and kissed it.

'I'll try to get away from here next year,' Sebastian mused. 'Too many disturbing undercurrents at the *Landestheater*.' He put his hand back on my breast.

'I don't know how I can ever tell my father my dream was just an air bubble . . .puff . . . and gone.'

'He loves you . . . he'll understand. Be glad you have him. I was ten when my father fell in the war. I didn't have a special relationship with him . . . I didn't adore him like you do yours. I always felt closer to my mother. Today I know how much I missed him while growing up. I like to listen to my mother talking about him - telling me stories about what we did together when I was a child. He became my hero. I meet him in my dreams now.'

The candle had burned down. Sebastian wrapped his arms around me and made love to me. Neither of us was as eager and as passionate as we had been the other times. We made love with affection and earnestness. We took our time. We looked into each other's eyes, and when finally he collapsed on my chest, we felt our breaths moving in unison.

Chapter 31

I felt calmer now – I knew Sebastian couldn't be with me, no need to wait for a knock on my door or to imagine a secret meeting at his place. His wife was with him. I wasn't jealous – I admired her. She had been able to capture a prince. How had she done it? I had to be content with catching a glimpse of him that night, our second-to-last *Beaver Coat* performance.

I went up to the stage earlier than usual – it would give me a chance to have a few words with him. Saying what? How's your wife? No, that I could never do! It would hurt him. I waited at our regular place in the wings. He didn't show up. I looked around. There was someone sitting on a prop behind the stage in the dark. Who was that? I went to look. Sebastian! It was him! He was sitting quite still, his head bent forward, his hands folded in his lap. When I stopped in front of him, he raised his head. He looked changed. There was an expression on his face I hadn't seen before. It frightened me.

'Sebastian, what's the matter? You look . . . tired.' My calmness had vanished, my heart was pounding.

'I had little sleep last night . . .' he mumbled – more to himself than to me.

'Oh sure, I understand . . .'

'It's not that, Annabel,' he looked into my eyes for the first time. 'Helga found some long dark hair in our bed.'

I felt a sharp stab in my chest. 'Oooh . . .' a muffled cry escaped my throat. 'Oh no . . .' I covered my mouth with my hand and stared into his eyes.

'Don't look so frightened, Annabel. It'll be fine . . . in time.'

I heard footsteps behind me.

'Annabel, your cue! Are you deaf?' The stage manager grabbed me and pushed me into the lights.

I knew my scene so well I could have performed it in my sleep. Only this time I didn't enjoy it. I had to look in the direction of Sebastian's entrance, and see him there, my beautiful, proud lover, now a bundle of misery. I wanted to hug him, comfort him, make him feel better, yet I didn't even dare touch his hand on my exit – the Snoop was lurking near by.

'*To die – to sleep – no more; and by a sleep to say we end the heartache, and the thousand natural shocks that flesh is heir to. . .*'

The words of Hamlet's famous soliloquy, etched into my mind in the voice of Lawrence Olivier, echoed in my head. To sleep – how could I possibly! The grey light of dawn was creeping into my room when finally the wheels in my head stopped turning, and nature took over. I awoke around noon, exhausted. A nightmare had held me in its claws, and hadn't allowed me to return to reality, a reality I didn't know how to face. It had been a repeat of my previous dream: Sebastian waiting for me on-stage, I don't know what play is on – I have no costume, no make-up on my face – I enter and find myself alone on stage, greeted by idiotic laughter. What was the meaning of that? Was the big bad wolf about to devour me?

I got dressed and made use of the one remedy that had helped me in the past – I went for a walk. I walked briskly through the town and followed the road into the country. I walked and walked. I didn't feel the tiredness in my legs only the pain in my broken heart. I needed to move on, farther and farther. The steeple of a church that peeked out from behind a field of high grass drew me close. I noticed a cross on top of the steeple. A Catholic Church! Werner's mother's church! How I had teased him about his mother's religious principles in regard to sex and marriage! Coming closer, I found myself in front of a small stone building with gothic windows. I looked at the carved wooden door. Would it be unlocked? Did I dare enter? Suddenly the door opened and an old woman appeared. She stepped out and held the door for me. I had to go in. I was confronted by a strange new smell. I looked around – half scared, half intrigued. Though the ornate candelabras in the nave weren't lit, the interior was bright enough to make out details. Light was streaming through plate-glass windows that were overflowing with bright, vivid colours. There was Mary and the infant Jesus, Saint George fighting the dragon, Jesus ascending to heaven surrounded by angels. My eyes moved to the paintings between the windows. The artist had painted them right onto the white-washed walls. They were simple pictures, like a child would paint – pastoral scenes with horses, sheep and shepherds. Their simplicity spoke to me. I walked up to the front and stopped before the altar. It was also a piece of art: three panels, carved out of wood, and painted in splendid colours. I was reminded of the church I had been confirmed in at home. It had coloured windows and an ornate altar as well. It had been built before the Reformation, our pastor used to tell us. I imagined him now preaching from the pulpit. He had the habit of moving his eyes around, making contact with each member of his congregation. I had always felt conscience-stricken when his glance fell on me. How would I be able to bear his gaze now?

Uuuuhmm . . . an enormous sound made me turn. I saw the back of a man in the gallery. He was facing the tall organ pipes. He made them moan and howl. I sat down in the nearest pew. The organ made the whole church reverberate – the building seemed too small to stand up to the power of the sound. I was reminded of Margaret's scene in the cathedral when the Evil

Spirit mocks her, because she gave herself to her beloved Dr. Faustus.

'*I feel like the organ is suffocating me,*' she says, '*the music is dissolving my heart . . .*' And the Evil Spirit answers, '*Hide, sin and shame will not stay hidden.*' Margaret feels her world collapse around her and faints.

How differently the sound of the organ affected me! It washed over me like a warm summer rain and released my troubled mind. I felt no guilt – just sadness. I knew our love affair had to be over. It didn't matter that I still wanted him, still loved him with all my heart. Tears flooded my eyes and I let them roll down my cheeks. I cried and cried. When the organ stopped, I dried my eyes and looked around. The light had fled. The only brightness came from a few candles flickering at the feet of a statue of Mary. I was drawn to it. A woman was kneeling on the little bench in front of the statue. She was young. Her eyes were closed, her lips were moving in prayer. Did she pray for a broken heart to heal? I wanted to kneel down beside her and pour out my heart to Mary. She had loved and suffered. What was my suffering compared to hers? How did I dare come to her with my pain, a pain I had brought on myself – had chosen for myself! Did I wish I hadn't loved Sebastian? Would I prefer our coming together hadn't happened? Oh no . . . no . . . a hundred times no! It'll be all right in time, Sebastian had said. How much time? How long would it take to calm my desire – how long?

Werner arrived and I managed to act like nothing worth mentioning had happened to me. I was glad to have him; I needed his friendship, his love. Only, how could I have sex with him? I wanted Sebastian. To postpone the inevitable, I questioned him, as soon as we had settled in my room, about the news he had for me, the news that was so important he hadn't wanted to tell me in his letter.

'I'll tell you,' he said, 'but please, Schatzi, hear me out before you reply, please Annabel.'

An uneasy feeling made me pick up one of the beer bottles I had bought, grab a couple of glasses, fill them up and take a good gulp.

'You make it sound so serious . . .'

'It is, it's very serious. I'm very serious. It's the most serious thing I'll ever do. Annabel, you need to tell me the truth . . .' Did he know? Had he found out about Sebastian and me?

'Don't torture me, Werner, what is it? Tell me!'

Werner took my hand and looked deep into my eyes. 'I want us to get married.'

'What . . .' I stared at him with an open mouth. My mind was scrambling to find a hold. My throat was so dry I downed another glass of beer.

'Annabel, what's the matter . . . speak . . . say something . . .'

Stay calm – make light Anna. I poured myself more beer and took another gulp.

'If this is a proposal why aren't you on your knees,' I grinned.

'Oh Schatzi, be serious. I know you don't think much of the institution of marriage, sure there are plenty of unhappy ones around, only ours would be different. We know each other, we know what the other likes, wants, enjoys . . . and hates. And best of all we share our love for the theatre. I can't imagine a couple more suited than the two of us.'

Keep up the light tone Anna . . . don't say anything that would hurt him . . . and seriously, wouldn't it be a good, simple solution?

'Now, Herr Helwig, this is all quite unexpected. You need to give me time to think it over.' I mimicked Bette Davis in one of her movies. She was hailed as a great American actress, not an import like Ingrid Bergman and Vivien Leigh, and I had gone to find out if her reputation was justified. Her behaviour in the film *Mr. Skeffingten* had reminded me of my early dream of running a salon where rich, influential men would come to adore me. How silly I had been! I wanted one man, just one – and it wasn't Werner. He, presently, was on a mission – not to be sidelined.

'I've put a deposit on a flat, ideal for the two of us, in a desirable area. When you stand on your toes in the bathroom you can see the Rhine! No more shared bathrooms, I know how you hate that, and a kitchen nook with stove and everything. You can cook up a storm, Schatzi.'

He was so excited I didn't have the heart to drown his dream. My brain, after all the beer I had drunk, had lost its edge – a pleasant feeling. Why not marry Werner? Marriage to him meant no more loneliness . . . his support in all I undertook . . . his kindness and his care . . . his steadiness . . . his reliability . . . but above all: the pain of seeing Sebastian without being able to have him – removed. With time the pain would get less, I had told myself. It would get less much faster if we were apart – if he were out of my life altogether.

'Schatzi, what are you thinking? Why don't you talk to me?'

Werner's mood had changed. He looked worried.

'No, seriously, I need time. I have just signed my new contract here. I have no idea what the almighty boss will say? How is he going to find a replacement that late in the season? And what will it do to my résumé?'

I had finished my third bottle of beer and as usual felt light and gay – and argumentative. My pain over Sebastian was losing some of its grip.

'Please let's not argue.' Werner pulled me close. 'You haven't even kissed me properly yet.'

Thanks to the quantities of beer I had consumed, I endured our love-making without suffering. Werner was quite tipsy as well and didn't notice my limited participation in the act.

'We'll talk more tomorrow,' he mumbled, sleep in his voice. 'You'll see it's the best thing for both of us.'

Chapter 32

I listened to Werner's breathing. I felt his warm body beside me, relaxed, peaceful. How did he manage to sleep at a time like this? I hadn't given him a positive answer – his future was also up in the air! And there he was, sleeping soundly – maybe he was having a wonderful dream? Oh Saint Anne, help me! What shall I do – what?

The careless, hazy feeling I had enjoyed thanks to the three bottles of beer had worn off. I was wide-awake. My mind was doing tumbling exercises like a gymnast. What was I going to do? Was Werner's proposal a gift from the good fairy or the ruin of my life? Sure, it'll be a relief to be away from the Queen Bee, who didn't appreciate me, from the Snoop, who stalked Sebastian, and from the Beerbelly, the Mata Hari of the *Landestheater*. But, above all, away from Sebastian! I couldn't imagine myself alone in my room at night and Sebastian so close. Or on stage acting as his partner . . . or waiting in the wings together . . . I would never be able to free myself of him! I would hope from one day to the next, from one look, one touch to the next, for a reunion. I would become a lovesick fool, and hate myself for it. No, I couldn't stay – it would be torture. I looked at Werner again, sleeping like a baby. When he stirred, I got up. I didn't want to have sex with him again, now that I was sober.

After breakfast, we went for a walk. I felt safe having him at my side, and I wanted the whole town to see us together. We went for coffee and Werner ordered two Cognacs – to celebrate our official engagement. I welcomed the soothing effect of the alcohol. Maybe the almighty boss had no intention of letting me go . . . he didn't have to . . . I had signed . . . maybe I didn't have to make a decision . . . maybe it would be made for me? I downed my second Cognac and the big fat knot that was strangling my brain loosened. It wasn't all up to me! And if I was let go without trouble, it was a sure sign they didn't really want me – with or without a lisp.

Werner had to leave the next morning and I promised him I would ask the great boss to release me.

'Tell him we are getting married and need to live together,' Werner said. 'He won't want to stand in our way, I'm sure.'

I should have felt triumphant when I asked the ruler of the enterprise to release me from my contract. Why didn't I? He, on the other hand, was pleased.

'You made the right decision, Fräulein Lambert. A young woman like you shouldn't be alone for the sake of a career. I'm sorry there is no vacancy for your fiancé here, I like to employ married couples, it makes for more stability in the ensemble . . .' he shifted some papers on his desk, 'and we mustn't forget, Lippburg is a small town, people talk . . .' He pulled down his glasses and looked into my eyes. I felt the blood rushing into my face. He knows . . . the Beerbelly has told him.

'Thank you for your kind understanding,' I said and rose to my feet. I wanted to get out, out before he could say another word. I was about to pull the door open and slip away when the all-powerful man got up, walked towards me and shook my hand.

'Congratulation Fräulein Lambert! I hope you'll be very happy.'

I felt tears filling my eyes. 'Thank you,' I mumbled. I turned and quickly closed the door behind me.

It was done! I convinced myself it was the right way to go – there was no other path I could take. The news about my departure was common knowledge the next day – my colleagues congratulated me on my engagement, my upcoming marriage. 'Are you going to give up acting?' my comedy father asked. I shook my head. 'Then you are in for it, Annabel. Do you have any idea how long actors' marriages last? It's the separation that kills them - and the temptations,' he winked. 'Don't believe our great boss – he doesn't like to engage married couples, few theatres do. It creates favouritism, jealousies and squabbles. Oh Annabel, you are such a lovely girl, watch out! Look after yourself.' I was raising my arms to hug him – no, stop! He'll notice that you are crying. I smacked a brief kiss on his cheek and ran away.

Why couldn't I just pack up and leave right away? There were three more performances for me, that's why, the last one *The Beaver Coat* in Bad Salzach.

I had so waited for that final performance to arrive. It would bring us together again, at least for that brief period in the wings. But Sebastian wasn't on the bus. Where was he? What had happened? As usual, the Beerbelly did a head count.

'Sebastian isn't here yet,' the Snoop piped up.

'He's riding over on his Vespa,' our director answered, 'he'll be there.'

He was, in the dark, in the wings, waiting – for me? We stood side by side . . . I smelled his aftershave . . . I looked at his beautiful profile . . . I had so wanted to see him . . . now I could hardly bear it! Sebastian looked around, then touched my hand.

'Meet me behind the church,' he whispered. 'I came on the Vespa so our director can't invite himself to my house when we get back . . .' The Snoop, like a ghost that can slide through walls, materialized at his side. ' . . . I hope you are going to be happy, Annabel, in your new adventure,' Sebastian pretended to finish his sentence.

I didn't know how I got on the bus, or to the place of our rendezvous. My mind was spitting out questions faster than a two-year-old child's! Why did he want to meet with me? What did he want to tell me? What had happened at his home? Was his wife going to leave him? Was he going to leave her because of me?

Sebastian was leaning against the church wall, in the shadow of the bell tower, when I arrived. He stepped forward and took me in his arms. My heart was pounding, my knees buckling; I wanted to crawl into him, to find a hold, a home in him. The bell struck midnight, twelve booming strokes. They gave me time to find myself, my strength. I became alert.

'Sorry we have to meet this way,' Sebastian whispered after the last stroke had died. 'I wanted to see you so I can say goodbye properly . . . I need to know you are alright . . . are you?'

The faint hope I had been harbouring collapsed with a bang. I wanted to flop down and cry. Instead I closed my eyes and focussed on my breathing. I managed to hang on.

'Oh sure,' I answered in my normal voice. 'I'll be fine . . .'

'And Werner, he's . . .'

'He doesn't know about us,' I said quickly and with an unexpected vehemence, 'and he doesn't need to.'

'Right,' Sebastian muttered, 'I agree.'

Some being must have been rooting for me – the good fairy or Saint Anne with the otherworldly smile? A calmness came over me. All I wanted at that moment was a good exit. I kept quiet.

'Werner is blessed to have you,' Sebastian's voice was soft and unsteady, 'under different circumstances . . .' he didn't finish his sentence. 'Here,' he pulled an envelope out of his pocket. 'This is for you. Open it when you are home. I needed to give you something – our time together . . .' His words were left hanging in the air. He suddenly was in a hurry. He kissed me but there was no passion in his kiss – and there wasn't any in my response either. I only felt sadness – like one would feel when a loved one dies.

Sebastian was gone. All that was left of him was the faraway hum of his Vespa. I sat down on one of the gravestones and allowed the floodgates to open. I cried my broken heart out. How long did I sit there, sobbing? I only know that my bum began to feel cold and damp. I got up and walked the few steps to my house. In my room, I tore open the envelope and unfolded a piece of paper. It was a poem in Sebastian's handwriting - he had composed a love poem for me! I read about the calmness of night . . . of peace and tranquility when the world sleeps . . . in Brahman's arms? It wasn't a love poem! It said nothing about me or our relationship! It was a poem by his revered Hermann Hesse that he had copied for me! Oh shit! Did he think that's what I needed at that moment? A realization struck me like a thump on the head: I didn't know him at all - or maybe I didn't mean much to him! My disappointment in his gift helped me to regain a good chunk of my senses. I was a lovesick fool! I had fallen once again for a handsome man and had taken his desire to sleep with me for love. At that moment of clarity I had only one desire: to get away! I remembered how fast my broken heart had healed after Daniel had disappeared from the school. He was now just a fond memory. I thanked the good fairy for him. I couldn't have had a more handsome, more charming, more gentle lover for my first sexual experience. Sebastian too would be a fond memory one day – one day, not yet! Oh, how I longed for him, how I wanted him! Enough! I dragged my suitcase out from under the eaves in the attic and started to pack. Home, I had a home! I had a place where I could recuperate, where my cracked heart could glue itself together, where my confused, tortured mind had a chance to rearrange itself. I longed to see my Papa.

The next day I knocked on my landlady's door to say goodbye. I hoped she wouldn't be in. I had prepared a thank-you note to slide under her door. No such luck! Peter opened the door. I assured his mother I had enjoyed my time in her house, and I would stay in touch – a kind lie. Peter insisted on accompanying me to the station and carrying my suitcase. We shook hands when the train rolled in.

'I'm glad you are marrying Herr Helwig,' Peter confessed. 'He's much more friendly than Herr Schoen.' I don't know what possessed me. I said, 'Herr Schoen is married, Peter.'

'That's what I mean . . .'

I was the one who blushed this time.

Chapter 33

The two hours on the train flew by as fast as the trees, the houses, and the cows I spotted through the window. I was busy. I wrote and rehearsed a scene I intended to produce at the station, during the car ride and at home, if necessary.

General mood – light, easy.

Father: Anna, I'm worried. Why did you leave the *Landestheater?*

Annabel: Werner and I are getting married, and we'll live together in Düsseldorf. He's found a lovely flat for us with a view of the Rhine (she smiles happily).

Father: (concerned) What will you live on? Neither of you has a contract for the new season.

Annabel: There are four theatres in Düsseldorf and many more in the Rhine/Ruhr area. Werner is in thick with the boss of the *Boulevard Theater*. He's arranged a meeting. The company is looking for a young woman to play the lead in a new comedy. (Annabel hugs her father, then dances around the dining table humming a tune.)

Father: I know they didn't treat you right in Lippburg . . . not the way you deserved. . . those two directors and their favouritism . . . still, you had a steady income . . . you might have made friends over time . . . (his voice trails off).

Annabel: I was lonely, Papa, and you know what that can lead to! Werner is a very caring person, and trustworthy, and . . . aren't you glad for us?

I was sure my Papa and my stepmama would be happy to see my relationship with Werner legitimized. Our sleeping together without a licence must have been bearing heavily on them for a long time.

My performance was admirable, I had to admit. I stuck to my script in the car, all the way to our home – just had to omit the dance around the table. At the house, my little sister, whose presence in my Papa's life I had so resented, saved me. Instead of getting into an adult conversation, I played with her. She loved doing peek-a-boo and screeched with joy when she discovered me behind the couch or under the table. She would hide by putting her hands over her eyes – her little mind thinking she was invisible that way. When she tired of that game, I pretended to be a dog, and barked at her. Right away she turned into a dog as well. So the two of us crawled around the furniture on all fours. I called her Fifi and showed her how to kneel and beg for treats. My Papa joined the game by feeding us biscuits and patting our heads. Little sister was babbling and yawping and wailing with pleasure. In the coming days she followed me around the house, gibble-gabbled at me, hugged me, and showed her appreciation of my playful presence by placing many wet kisses on my cheeks. Clara, my parents had named her, like the girl in the Nutcracker tale. She was about as fearless as her namesake! I just had to love her.

But I wasn't out of the deep dark pit of my broken heart's pain. And my Papa wasn't going to be fooled for long. So far, I had avoided being alone with him – it wasn't hard with Clara around. At night, I made sure the radio was on. Papa liked to listen to the news – my stepmama to a play or a concert. When the program was over, it was late, and Papa was ready to turn in. One night though Mama excused herself, and went to bed early. My father didn't waste a minute.

'Anna, what's the matter? You look tired and you have lost weight – and I can't find the spark in your eyes that I used to love. Is it Werner – are you not sure about the marriage?'

'Oh sure I'm sure . . . he'll always care for me . . . you don't need to worry . . .' I sputtered out the words without thinking.

'Do you love him, Anna . . . I haven't heard you say that . . . I haven't heard you talk about him . . . I don't see the exuberance in you that goes with wedding plans. Anna, are you sure you are doing the right thing? Are you sure you want to be with Werner for the rest of your life? Or is there someone else?'

I had been holding my breath, I noticed, now I exhaled. I couldn't tell him about Sebastian – my Papa's belief in me would be crushed. But I couldn't continue to play my game either. I had to get away fast before I broke down and spilled my whole, miserable story.

'Sorry, Papa, I'm not feeling well tonight, just the monthly thing . . .' I got up too fast and flew out of the room. I closed my bedroom door with too much bang, threw myself on my bed, punched my pillow, then buried my face in it and sobbed like a child whose favourite toy is lost. I drowned my pain over Sebastian in a river of tears.

After some time, I don't know how long, I felt a hand on my back, stroking gently. I turned my wet face and there was my stepmama, sitting on the bed beside me, stroking me.

'He broke your heart . . . didn't he? Oh my poor Anna . . .' she didn't look into my eyes just kept stroking.

'You . . . know?'

'Your brother told me. He had surprised you two when he visited unexpectedly, remember?'

'Oh no! What does Papa . . .'

'We didn't tell him Anna, don't worry. Hans and I have become close. He loves to complain to me about Christa – something your father doesn't tolerate. Your Papa tells him that he expects his son to show respect and understanding for his wife. But I know how it is – their temperaments are not well matched. It helps Hans to share his marital problems with me.'

'I keep thinking of Sebastian all the time . . . I can't help it . . . I miss him so . . . we were so happy together . . . I was sure he loved me. . .' It felt so good to pour out my heart to her, to spill all that locked-up misery – to have someone to confide in!

'It sounds presumptuous, but I know how you feel. My heart was broken when my fiancé was killed in the war. I was sure I would never be able to love another man. For three years I grieved for him. Oma started to tease me . . . she had a date every weekend by then . . . my father had died early in their marriage you know, and during the war there was little chance for her to find a new husband. I guess she was making up for lost time. I had a brief relationship with an American sergeant . . . I knew from the beginning there wasn't a chance to make it permanent. When I met your father it was the opposite: I knew he was my man. I fell head over heels for him.'

'I didn't know you had been engaged before.'

'Oh ja . . . and on Harry's last furlough we spent every day and every night together. When I got the notice of his death, it was a comfort to me to know that by our coming together, married or not, his short life had been more complete.'

'I don't really know much about you, Mama. I'd love to learn more.'

'You were so young when your father and I married. You had just turned fourteen. Sure, some girls start to date at that age – not you! You were a child, as innocent as Clara is. I'm guilty of not educating you in sexual matters. Forgive me. First,

I felt it wasn't my place, you being so close to your Papa. Later, I simply trusted you to know – and so did your father. Quite foolish of us.'

'It wouldn't have made any difference, Mama, I would still have fallen for the wrong men . . . for handsome, charming, kind and intelligent men. Why do you think that is?'

'Maybe because your father has all the attributes you just mentioned.'

'You're so right!' I had to laugh. 'He's all that – just very principled where out-of-wedlock sex is concerned!'

For the first time in ages I had a long, deep sleep. Just before I snuggled into Morpheus' arms, I contemplated my fairy tale education. In regard to stepmothers, the Brothers Grimm had been spreading highly exaggerated beliefs. Not all of them were bad witches. As a matter of fact, mine was pretty terrific.

Chapter 34

I had to make a decision – and soon! Mama and I sat up late the following night, while my darling Papa turned in early – on purpose I'm sure. He knew there was something going on that didn't require his input, something that had brought Mama and me closer together. He was pleased – I saw it in his eyes. He trusted his wife to get things sorted out to my advantage.

Mama fetched a bottle of wine from the cellar and kept refilling my glass, while I poured out my lovesick heart shedding sufficient tears to fill a swimming pool. Mama was patient – just listened to my babbling. Midnight had passed when suddenly I got tired of my whining and my waffling. My brain kicked in like somebody had flicked a switch: I couldn't marry Werner! The words the Hawk had spoken more than two years ago popped out of my memory. 'Werner is not enough for you,' he had said. After knowing Sebastian, in particular in the biblical sense, I had to agree with him. Good old Hawk – good old soothsayer. How well he had known me! I wasn't ready to settle for what Werner and I had. And it wasn't fair to Werner either. He didn't deserve to be second choice. He had been good to me, loving and caring – but not enough! Maybe, above all, fairy tales, romantic novels and films had spoiled me. I knew my adventure wasn't over yet. There were still riddles to be solved, pleasures to be found, fire and fury to be endured. I wasn't ready to settle for security and comfort.

I enjoyed being home, now that I had found a friend in my stepmama and an appreciative audience in my little sister. Any grimace, any change in my voice amused her. 'Do dat again,' she would call out when a particular impression pleased her. She filled the house with noise, motion, and joy – and kept my Papa on his toes. She was a fountain of youth for him.

One day my darling Papa came home from the office carrying a small, portable typewriter. 'I got you an early birthday present, Anna. I thought you might want to write some applications.'

'It's too late, Papa, all subsidized theatres have finished hiring a long time ago.'

'What about writing to your agent then – aren't you keen on trying out this great little machine?'

Darling, darling Papa! Thanks to his gift and his casual suggestion I got a contract after all. Or was the good fairy looking out for me because I had made a brave decision – I had decided to battle my future on my own? I got hired because a 'one in a million' event had happened in Hanover. A young actress of my genre had married during the summer break – a proper count of the Hapsburg line. She had said goodbye to her career and moved with him to the family estate in Austria. I noticed a flicker of hope in my Papa's eyes when he learned of the circumstances that had led to my late employment. There was a faint chance, still a chance, that his daughter might meet and marry a man of status – and enjoy all the trimmings that went with it. No wonder I was such a romantic! It was a matter of genes!

My first part in Hanover, Angélique in Molière's *Le Malade Imaginaire*, introduced me to eight new male colleagues. Three were old, two middle-aged, three young. Two of the latter were in love with me – in the play. Only one was good-looking. He was tall, had straight dark hair, and a good face for a young hero. But he was so full of himself that I was turned off right away. Absolutely not my type! Reminded me of Remus in Cleves – loudmouthed and opinionated. No danger of falling in love with him! No danger of falling in love with anybody. I loved Sebastian! At night, in my lonely bed, I dreamed of him. I remembered his kisses, the way he had stroked my breasts, had moved his hands over my tummy, and slowly lower down, ever so gently, and how he had made me look into his eyes at the height of our passion. There had been something . . . something so out-of-this-world in our coming together . . . time had stood still. Oh Sebastian, I missed you so!

The men of power at my new employ, three directors and the almighty top man, were friendly towards me in a casual, uncommitted way. I didn't mind that because the director of *Le Malade* took me under his wings. He was the first man who ever worked on a part with me. I mean, talked to me about the role, corrected my diction, smoothed out my movements, and took his time helping me become Angélique. She, as he pointed out, wasn't just a young girl – she was a girl brought up in a seventeenth-century household, a child of her time. What a new perspective he opened up! I felt blessed. My heart was brimming with gratitude. The time he spent with me on the part, without showing the slightest interest in my flesh, gave me confidence in myself and in the choice of my profession. For the first time in a long while I realized how creative, exciting, and all-absorbing my profession was. I was allowed to transform myself with every new part. I was allowed to make people laugh or cry, dream or swear. Was there a more rewarding way to make a living?

I have to admit I found myself in a tunnel of darkness from time to time. A great sadness would come over me when I noticed a couple of lovers, oblivious to the world around them, in the park. It wasn't solely Sebastian I missed – Werner had left a big emptiness in my emotional reservoir as well. His reliable presence, his support and his love that I had taken for granted, were gone. I had hoped there would be a Donata or a Hanna in the ensemble – no such luck. I was alone. After long contemplation and a good talking to myself, I started lessons with a voice teacher – not to correct my lisp – there wasn't one! My angel director encouraged me to take singing and dancing lessons as well. 'American musicals will soon crowd the German stages,' he told me. 'You'd better be prepared.' I was in full agreement. My singing voice, if I had one, needed to be coaxed to life. With all this activity, my loneliness flew right out of the window.

I had made another decision: I wasn't going to be an outsider again. Never mind how much Sebastian had liked it that I kept to myself, I was going to belong to a popular clique for a change. It was hard work. I went to all first night-parties, hung around the theatre after rehearsal, went for lunch with some of my colleagues, listened to their gossip and tried to come up with some of my own. Result: I went broke and often felt uncomfortable in my own skin. I was a one-on-one person, likely spoiled by all the attention my darling Papa had lavished on me when I was a child – darn it!

We had been working on *Le Malade* for three weeks. I was walking to my room after a late rehearsal. A Vespa, parked on the sidewalk in front of my house, caught my eye. My heart jumped – silly! There are a thousand Vespas in a city as large as Hanover, I told myself – so my dear heart, stop the gymnastics. I unlocked the front door and stepped into the hall. A beam of light came from my landlady's partly open parlour door – and the smell of fresh coffee. I stood still. She was talking with great animation, and giggled like a young girl between sentences.

Whom did she entertain at this hour? I stepped closer – a voice. . . *the* voice . . . it couldn't be . . . was I going mad? I knew this voice, I could pick it out among hundreds . . . this deep, warm, melodious voice . . . Sebastian's voice! I stepped into the light of the room and like a prince in a fairy tale, Sebastian materialized.

'We have been waiting for you, Fräulein Lambert. Your friend told me all about your relationship.' Frau Schreiner greeted me with a smile.

'Helloo . . .' the only word I was capable of producing hung in the air.

'Hello, Annabel . . .' Sebastian shook my hand. 'I have a day off . . . I wanted to see you . . .'

'You needn't be so formal, you two. Anybody can see what you feel for each other . . .' Frau Schreiner must have gone on talking – I didn't hear her anymore. I just wanted to take Sebastian up to my room, hug him and kiss him and be held by him and love him . . . love him.

I tuned into the conversation again when my landlady said, 'It's all right, Herr Schoen, you can stay here with Annabel. I'm not one of those old fashioned, out-of-touch-with-the-times kind of person. Lovers belong together, that's my philosophy.'

'Thank you, Frau Schreiner, thank you . . .' I stuttered, and before she could start the conversation again, I took Sebastian by the hand and pulled him out of the room. He grabbed a rucksack that lay in the hall and we raced up the stairs, only one flight now, and slipped into my room.

Sebastian pulled me into his arms and kissed me.

'Annabel, Liebling, are you glad I came . . . I had to, you know . . . I had to see you . . . talk to you. . .'

'Don't,' I said, 'no need to talk. Just hold me.'

Did it take minutes or seconds? We were in bed, under the covers, loving each other, wallowing in each others' physical presence, oblivious to anything else.

I had rehearsal in the morning. Sebastian was going to wait in my room for my return. 'I have to talk to you. Come back soon,' he mumbled when I left – still half-asleep. He had to be back in Lippburg at seven at the latest to get ready for his performance. A two, maybe three-hour-drive lay ahead of him.

I was physically present on the rehearsal stage at nine, my mind was not. The events of last night delighted, puzzled, confused me. I had been sure I would never see Sebastian again, unless we accidentally bumped into each other at some special theatre event. And now he had come back to me – why? He had to talk to me – what about? The delight I had felt at seeing him turned into fear. Was I going to see him again after he left – and when? Was my mind going to be all stirred up again – my career jeopardized by my longing for him? Oh my good fairy, my blessed Saint Anne, give me strength!

'Annabel, where are you? May I ask you to participate in our scene?' My angel director jerked me into the present. 'I know you have no text at the moment but I expect you to react to your colleagues' dialogue . . . show some emotion . . . it's a comedy . . . you look like you've just returned from a funeral!'

'Sorry,' I muttered, 'I'm so sorry . . .'

I was back home with Sebastian at noon. A tray with dishes and a coffeepot was sitting on the table. Dear open-minded Frau Schreiner had made breakfast for him. Sebastian kissed me and sat me down on a chair. I was glad, my legs felt wobbly.

'Listen to me Annabel . . . I said yesterday I have to tell you something. I waited because I needed to know first that you wanted me . . . that there was no change in your heart. Helga and I are getting a divorce . . . no, don't look so guilty, you're not the reason . . . my wife has become close to a man she works with in Düsseldorf. It was a joint decision to split up . . . there had been too much separation.'

And too much temptation, I couldn't help thinking.

'Annabel, Liebling . . . I know you love me . . . I'll soon be free . . . will you marry me?'

I heard the organ playing the Wedding March, I felt my prince lifting me on his white horse, I saw the beautiful castle gleaming in the distance, I opened my mouth and heard myself say:

'NO.'

No? Where did that come from? After a silence of what seemed hours, it dawned on me. In my heart of hearts, contrary to what the Brothers Grimm had told me, I had never believed that Cinderella and the prince lived happily ever after.

Acknowledgments

A heartfelt thank you goes to my friend Tim (Thelma Irvine) for her encouragement and her patience when my ignorance in the mysterious workings of Microsoft Word stopped me cold. Thank you Ejner for always answering my calls for help with the technology without delay.

Brigitte Roick was born in Germany. Her two years of study at the Max-Reinhardt-Schule in Berlin were followed by seven years of employment in professional theatre.

After making Canada her home, she obtained a Bachelor of Arts Degree from McMaster University and a Diploma in Early Childhood Education. Her studies in creative writing led to the publication of two of her short stories in the Anthology of the McMaster Certificate in Writing Program 2000. Her first novel, MOONCHILD, is available from www. trafford.com and all major book web sites.

www.ingramcontent.com/pod-product-compliance
Lightning Source LLC
Chambersburg PA
CBHW020613310726
48979CB00008B/1468/J

* 9 7 8 1 4 2 6 9 0 0 8 5 3 *